ALSO BY NELSON GEORGE

NIGHT WORK

A NOVEL

Nelson George

A TOUCHSTONE BOOK
Published by Simon & Schuster
NEW YORK   LONDON   TORONTO   SYDNEY   SINGAPORE

Dedicated to
the vampires of New York City
and
the lovely way they bite

TOUCHSTONE
Rockefeller Center
1230 Avenue of the Americas
New York, NY 10020

TOUCHSTONE and colophon are registered trademarks of
Simon & Schuster, Inc.

Designed by Colin Joh

Manufactured in the United States of America

ISBN 0-7394-3507-8

Three Times as Many Doors

In New York City there are at least three
times as many doors as people. Front doors to
homes and apartments. Back doors to alleys
and driveways. Doors to restaurants. Doors to
clubs and bars. Doors to brownstones and ten-
ements, to sitting rooms and dayrooms and
night rooms (also known as bedrooms). And
there are doors inside doors—doors to other
doors and other realities, doors to the rooms
where you expose yourself, where you embrace
the things you love so dearly you share them
with only a well-chosen few. I work behind
those closed doors, places where what happens
is just between the people there and no one
else has to know. I work in darkness even
when the light is on. You see, my name is
Night and I do night work.

Like Curtis Mayfield sang, "Dark as the
night with the moon shining bright." I'm as
dark as Michael Jordan or Tyson Beckford.
Smooth and black and glowing. Sometimes I
look at myself naked in the mirror above my
bed and watch how the light bounces off my
skin, how it reflects the curves and muscles

God gave me, and I smile at my ebony beauty.

I didn't always appreciate the chocolate. For much of my life my color was a curse, a burden, a target. It was all people saw. Nobody paid attention to my eyes, my mouth, or my troubled soul. I was a dot. I was midnight. I was doo-doo. I was black magic. I was blackmail. I was the black that existed to define white, yellow, and red. I was the punch line that made a sentence a joke. I was the exclamation point that made a sentence an insult. I was the nightmare that ruined dreams.

Black mothers laughed at me and kept their children at bay. White teachers joked about me over coffee and cigarettes. Schoolmates held up black crayons next to my face and told me I was darker. And my father—that evil fool—used to tell me I looked my best with the lights out.

Now my sister, she's yellow. "Yellow as a Chinaman's piss." That's what our father often said. But skin color never mattered between Nikki and me. When I'd be called "African looking" by a black person who hated himself or Sambo by someone who didn't care about history, it was Nikki who held my head and said, "One day they'll all love you like I do." I wanted to believe her but didn't. My sick little sis thought she could hear the

sound of stars and the heavy breathing of
fish in the aquarium, which didn't really
make her the most reliable source for life-
affirming information.

When I was a boy in Brooklyn I'd look
into our bathroom mirror, not in admiration
but pain. I used to stand over the sink and
rub my skin, expecting that it would all
appear like dirt in streaks on the pinkish
yellow palms of my hands. But it wouldn't
peel off. I'd think of Michael Jackson, the
boy-man who was so large during my childhood.
He'd made himself into science fiction by
shedding layers of skin as I so wanted to.
This should have been the perfect solution—to
shred it all and escape my burden, to quiet
all the talk and the nasty laughter and,
maybe, make my father love me.

The problem was what lay beneath. For
Michael there was a ghost face unlike anything I, or anyone else, had ever seen. His
black skin had withered and no amount of soul
singing could bring it back. And the light
from cracks under Michael's closed doors
caught my attention. Stripped of his skin and
his secrets, Michael was too naked, too damaged and damaging, for me to follow his path
any longer. This I could not envy. It was too
much. Too ugly. In fact, Michael's face
finally put me in check. No way could I allow

everyone else's poison in me. I began to
understand that my skin had to be loved if I
was to love myself.

So the day I turned sixteen I became
Night and I reclaimed my face.

And just in time, help arrived. Big Daddy
Kane, who was "big just like your Daddy,"
dropped "Raw." And Michael Jordan, who folk
in North Cacalacki used to call "the man in
the dark suit," before he sliced the Celtics
for sixty-something one Sunday afternoon. And
Wesley Snipes, who said, "Always bet on
black," and so I did. These brothers, and
others, helped reinvent the world around me.
They made everyone look at dark skin. I'm
talking about hi-top fade. I'm talking about
Jordan in Nike ads. I'm talking about Wes
boning in *Mo' Better* and Wes killing in *New
Jack City*. I'm talking bald brown domes
sweating under the sun. Dark skin in white
tank tops. Even Grace motherfucking Jones and
her freaky ass self. Black was back, all in,
we're gonna win. Night had been intended to
be my shield. Then things changed and it
became a sword.

"WHAT DO YOU NEED?"

It was around 10:30 A.M. when my cell phone rang. I opened my eyes and saw myself naked in the overhead mirror. I watched myself and debated answering. Most people know better than to call that early, so I figured it had to be family. Turned out to be the only person in my world who really mattered.

"What do you need?" I said. I tried to speak soulfully but my usual roughness broke through.

My sister, Nikki, replied, "I'm all right," which was clearly a lie.

"You're not all right, all right," I explained to her.

"I am all right," she replied petulantly. "I hate when you talk to me like this. I am not an invalid."

Nikki was twenty years old, had breasts the size of melons, and juggled a couple of low-rent boyfriends. Still, though technically a woman, Nikki spoke with the wavering cadence of a fourteen-year-old giving a school speech, which irritated me, though it was understandable. After all, little sis had been through too much.

"I'm sorry. I just want you to be taken care of." I spoke deliberately, trying to sound like I imagined a concerned father would. "You deserve to be taken care of. So let me do that, okay? Okay?"

Nikki sighed, said, "Okay," and waited for me to offer help once more.

"What do you need? You need money?"

"No," she said. "But can you come with me to the doctor today?"

"What time?"

"At four, I have to have a checkup. My headaches have been bad these last two weeks. I was supposed to go in next month but I moved it up. I'd like you to be there. Can you?"

This was already going to be a long, busy day for me. I'd been making moves for months to get it set up. My plan was to rest this morning, make some paper, and then get my body ready for the real work tonight. I needed some time to myself. But Nikki needed me, too.

I told her, "I'll be there. I have a lot of appointments later, but I'll be there."

"Appointments, huh." She grunted her disdain and I

ignored it. "Anyway, Martha's gonna drop me off. Figure I'll get a cab back."

"I'll meet you in the lobby at Bellevue around a quarter to."

"Thank you, big brother."

"Anything for you, baby girl. Know that."

I lay in bed and made a mental map of my day. Uptown, downtown, uptown, down. Maybe it wouldn't be so bad if I lived in a midtown condo. Everything would be kinda close. But I lived in the East Village, on a block halfway between yuppie heaven and ghetto hell. A shotgun apartment with a shower in the kitchen, a toilet in the back of the place, and all the charm of the immigrant squat it was way back in the day. Wasn't even near the iron horse. Lots of cabbies still thought there were junkies in Tompkins Square Park. Still, it was my piece of this co-op building and I didn't have a roommate, so I was doing all right. All I had to do was finish my demo, get just a little more cheddar, and I'd have my midtown condo real soon.

Turned on the radio to NewsRadio 88 so I could be up on what was going on. The weatherman said that today was the winter solstice, the shortest day of the year. Which meant it was also the longest night of the year. I sat up in bed. I looked up at the mirror nailed to my ceiling and studied my groin. Shit, I was still the longest Night that I knew.

I'D BEEN SERVING HER ABOUT A YEAR

Frank Bacon-Robinson, a prominent Negro business-man, active Democrat, and civil-rights-era leader, died about two years back. I'd been serving his white widow, Shirley, for about a year. It was from her, actually, that I learned a lot about Dr. King, the Freedom Riders, and a lot of stuff about the civil rights movement my father had derided.

Mrs. Bacon-Robinson lived in one of those huge Central Park West apartments with a spectacular view of Manhattan and seemingly endless rooms. In what used to be her husband's den, Shirley set up an exercise room with a StairMaster, light weights, and spongy floor mats. On the walls were posters: Dr. King at the March on Washington; Muhammad Ali standing over Sonny Liston and screaming in triumph; Michael Jordan dunking on some unworthy NBA fool; Bob Marley singing; Malcolm X gesturing during a speech.

It was a white room decorated with black male hero-ism. And it was in that room I decorated Mrs. Bacon-

Robinson's petite alabaster body with my mahogany
skin. I came over once, maybe twice a month in the
guise of a personal trainer, one of my favorite covers.
Often Mrs. Bacon-Robinson and I screwed atop one of
the floor mats, but when inspired I'd prop her rail-thin
body against the wall and let her little legs dangle over
my ass, pumping away right next to Dr. King's vision of
racial harmony. I do believe Mrs. Bacon-Robinson was
actually at that march in '63 and, due to the wonders of
modern science, didn't look a day over forty-five.

Sometimes, as we screwed, I'd look up at King's face
and wonder whether my client was one of the women
on J. Edgar Hoover's FBI surveillance tapes. Maybe I
was hitting one of Dr. King's exes. It was such an ill
thought it made me horny—anything like that was good
for getting me through the job. Sometimes mid-stroke I'd
ask Mrs. Bacon-Robinson if she'd been one of the great
man's "supporters," and she'd just close her eyes and
blood would flush her waxy face.

The truth was, I was a walking, dick-swinging stereotype, the kind of black male image the civil rights movement had had to overcome in order to succeed. What I
did was fucked up. I knew that. But then, everybody's
got something going on behind closed doors. Even Dr.

King had gotten his groove on. I justified the gig by telling myself this was my strange little contribution to twenty-first-century American race relations. I really hadn't known much about white people until I started sleeping with them. I knew about racism and I knew about hockey and I knew the president was always white and most people in prison were black—you know, the general stuff.

However, it wasn't until I was peeing in their bathrooms, leafing through their photo albums, and watching how much they enjoyed going barefoot, even on New York's dirty streets, that I got any real insight. First of all, I found that white people aren't as evil as my father used to preach. The average Caucasian isn't part of the white world conspiracy to dominate, intimidate, and subjugate people of color. To me they are, just like me, pawns in the American money game. All they really care about is feeding and clothing themselves and their offspring, buying high-status material goods, and living as well as TV tells them to. Jamal and James aren't that different. Within limits, many (but not as many as black folks often think) white folks are interested in, inspired by, and will pay money to be involved with our funky ass culture.

But mostly I find they don't think about us very much. You can tell this because when confronted with talk of race, white folks usually don't have the vocab. In post-sex conversations with white women, I find they usually speak in liberal or conservative clichés right off talk shows or, probably worse, like they know everything about black folks based on having had relations with brothers like me—"me" not exactly being representative of the overall values of the African-American community. It strikes me that most white folks have impressions of black folks but not true convictions, and that they often mistake the two. (Of course, the women who utilize my services ain't the average white women either.)

In America the intimate mix of sex and race are our unspoken history, and me, well, I make my living in the closeted desire created by that history. In essence I am a living breathing genuine Negro experience. I am cheaper than a safari, more professional than Amateur Night at the Apollo, and a lot more fun than a music video. One day, when everybody is as blended as the population of Brazil, my job description will disappear (though if I were you I wouldn't hold my breath).

But speaking in generalities is always dangerous. For example, what Mrs. Bacon-Robinson needed from me, fantasized about, and locked doors to enjoy was very, very specific. Always after intercourse Mrs. Bacon-Robinson and I retired to her spotless white bathroom, where the enamel glistened from the sweat of Dominican housekeepers, and we'd climb into the shower and clean each other as lovingly as our imaginations allowed. Every day of their life together, Frank and Shirley had washed each other. That ritual, some kind of marriage sacrament, had so defined Shirley's life that she couldn't live without it. On some visits the sex would be brief, just enough to work up a sweat, and then we'd retire to the shower. She scrubbed my back and I wiped behind her small ears. In that shower we were as intimate as I could fake it.

Afterward we sat in her living room, having tea and looking out at the green glory of Central Park.

"Do you think I'm strange, Night?" she asked.

"Strange. Hell, no. I know lots of strange people."

"I bet you do."

"And you're not one. You know what Spike Lee said?"

"No," she said, searching her mind for the politically correct cultural reference. "I mean, I know he's very controversial, so I'm not sure what statement you mean."

"His first movie was called *She's Gotta Have It*, and he

was right. That's just human nature. We all gotta have it."

"What about you, Night? Do you gotta have it?"

"Of course, Shirley. That's why I'm here."

"Oh, Night. Thank you, but I'm not senile yet. We both know why you're here, though I do like to be flattered."

"Don't worry, Shirley. I'm gonna get mine. And it starts tonight."

"Good, Night," she said, looking at me a little amused. "Good for you."

I picked up the beige monogrammed SBR envelope left next to my teacup, felt the hundred-dollar bills inside, and gave Shirley a soft kiss on the lips. I exited the building via the service door and then walked down Central Park West toward Columbus Circle. After my session with Shirley, it was time for a visit with my own personal trainer.

I Wanted to Be a Gigolo

When I was a teenager I realized I wanted to be a gigolo, though I had no idea the profession had a name. I just thought having women pay you for sex seemed like a good idea. Wasn't until I picked up that Richard Gere movie, *American Gigolo,* that I saw this was a real job. Gere played a character named Julian Kaye, a supersuave Beverly-Hills-Brentwood-Armani-clad-several-language-speaking pleasure-giver. He got pleasure giving pleasure.

Julian said his satisfaction didn't come from the fucking itself but from the idea that he made these women happy. I didn't really understand that distinction when I was younger, but I totally get it now. For Gere's character, it wasn't just about sex—it was clever convo, knowing antiques, and humming Smokey Robinson while folding pastel shirts. Seemed like a legitimate career path to me.

My port of entry was stripping. When I was nineteen my girlfriend, Anasette, started stripping at this midtown spot, Leg's Diamond. By day she took classes in nutrition at

Brooklyn College, and most nights she swung
her ass from a pole on Forty-fifth Street.
I'd pick her up as often as I could, trying
to keep the customers and the doorman off her
sweet cinnamon-colored butt.

One night Anasette told me one of the
club's promoters, a chubby fey Rican named
Ramon, had been asking about me. Told
Anasette I was handsome; wanted to know if I
had a six pack and a big dick. Just before
the doorman pulled me off that sloppy pink
faggot, the man offered me a gig.

A couple of Saturday nights after that,
I was onstage at a bingo hall on Flatbush
Avenue filled with feisty, roly-poly sisters
of Southern American and Caribbean stock,
dancing in green neon Speedos to Jay-Z's
"Can I Get A . . ." The crowd was wild—
WWF-level mania amongst women with soprano
voices and nasty, filthy mouths. I came on
early in the night dressed as a New York
Knick and made $350 in fives, tens, and one
fifty that someone stuck right between my
ass cheeks.

Then I watched as guys came on with
sequined suits, see-through boxers, and
remixes of Southern hip-hop and socca so raw
some women got red-faced even as they waved
ten-dollar bills. At the men's strip clubs
where Anasette toiled, the men often seemed

comatose, like the sight of all those swinging tits and swaying hips had paralyzed them.
They were mostly blank faced and sad and even
mean. It was like, instead wanting to get
busy, their desire for the strippers made
them angry and their dicks limp. I still
don't understand it, but it is what it is.

At these women's events it was like these
ladies had just gotten out of a female prison
and hadn't had a man in years. They wanted to
be served, and served well. Some wanted to be
teased. Some wanted to be obeyed. Some wanted
to be a heroine in a romance novel. A great
many just wanted to be humped like they
hadn't been boned in years (or maybe ever).
Hey, you don't come to a male-oriented strip
show looking for kindness, courtesy, or sensitivity. They came seeking the raw, wearing
tight slacks with their bulging bellies out,
nails polished like well-shined shoes, and
their babies tucked out of sight.

You had to give the ladies a show. None
of that walking around yawning that females
can get away with at a men's strip club. You
had to have a concept in order to make money,
like in *The Full Monty* or the Village People.
That's why I was a Knick. I wore the uniform;
the warm-ups, sneakers, and I even brought a
ball out with me as a prop. Most of the experienced guys had elaborate remixes, props,

and dance routines as if these were ghetto
Broadway shows.

It was in this environment that I got my
introduction to the gigolo life. Women would
jockey for position after the show. Bling
bling women with their Big Poppa's money.
Bureaucratic mommas with condos and Lexus
rides. Welfare mothers who didn't have much
material to offer but lots of enthusiasm. At
first I didn't partake. Number one, I had a
fine ass girlfriend. Number two, despite all
my fantasizing about being a gigolo, I was
young enough to find a lot of the women
frightening. To see them go so crazy and then
sweat me so hard at first kinda scared me—the
key phrase being "at first."

I was mentored through all this by J-Luv,
a pretty, pecan-colored Dominican who resembled the soap opera stud Shemar Moore minus
the acting job. J-Luv was a star on the
ghetto strip circuit that you found in the
BK, the Boogie Down, Harlem, and clubs in
Long Island and Newark.

"See my Jeep," he told me when we first
met. "See my watches? See how pretty my teeth
are? I don't pay for shit, dog. As long as I
keep my shit tight, I never will. Do as I
tell you and you can live like me."

I wasn't sure why he wanted to help me.
If I started clocking, it could mean less

cheddar for him or fewer gigs. I wasn't sure
if he was sweet or not, but I needed the
schoolin', and whether they loved me or hated
me, people always paid attention. So I just
listened and watched my ass.

We did a couple of gigs together before
J-Luv really peeped me to how to handle my
biz one night at a community center in Bed-
ford-Stuyvesant. When I came offstage, J-Luv
pointed at a heavyset woman in a beige off-
the-rack Macy's pants suit. The woman had
short-cropped black hair, small diamond earrings, and a nice watch. J-Luv told me, "I've
been watching her. Her face lit up when you
danced. Not just straight-up fuck lust but
like you were some dream she had, ya know?" I
didn't, but I nodded. He continued, "Go out
with her after the show. Don't say much. Listen or act like you're listening. Smile a
lot, and whatever you do, don't fuck her."

"That part's easy," I replied, and J-Luv
smiled.

"You already got a real good understanding of this, dog," he said admiringly. "Put a
little time in the game and you'll be living
at Trump Tower and not paying for shit."

Florence DeForest owned two apartment
buildings, three grocery stores, two travel
agencies, and some land down in her native
Antigua. Her industrious Jamaican husband had

run off with a clerk at one of the grocery
stores, and Florence hired a mean Fifth
Avenue divorce attorney to exact financial
revenge. Picking up well-constructed man meat
like me was either a continuation of that
vengeance or some attempt to reconnect to her
sexual self.

I think more the latter than the former.
The longer I didn't fuck her, the more gifts
came my way: a Rolex, an Armani suit, a gold
bracelet. All for three dinners, real quiet
conversation, and a couple light kisses and a
softly said "Good night." It was strange how
it worked and how easy I found the flow. I
danced. I teased. If I was a girl you could
have called me a cocktease.

The more I teased Florence the more this
businesswoman valued me. And the more Florence valued me, the more other women did,
too.

About six months after we met, J-Luv
introduced me to the world of private house
parties, where swinging couples brought in
dancers to get their fires started. The tips
could be amazing, but there's no guarantee,
especially if it was an older crowd where the
husbands inhibited the wives. Plus, having
ancient old biddies clawing at your arms,
slobbering on your chest, and if you're not
careful, sticking their bony fingers up your

ass kinda made me sick. Unlike a club where
there are bouncers, a stage, and a controlled
performance environment, at private parties
people treat you like a new toy.

This was particularly true of the gay
parties I did, which for me were out-of-body
experiences. Wearing leather shorts and a
matching tank top, I'd walk into a room full
of horny guys. The crowd would be dotted with
men bigger and buffer than me, with lust in
their eyes (and a boner in their tight-ass
jeans). It scared the hell out of me, but you
pulled down several grand per party, so when
J-Luv started asking me if I was down, I
couldn't say no.

Gay men have a woman's eye for masculine
beauty and a man's general lack of self-con-
trol, which meant these guys would grab you
and try to hump you every chance they had.
I've heard gory tales of dancers having
trains run on them in the back bedroom of a
gay men's party. I'm not being antigay here,
folks, but men—whatever their sexual orienta-
tion—are still men. So whenever I did gay
gigs, I danced sexy but I kept my eyes open
and my butt cheeks closed.

The money was always phat, but later I'd
have nightmares of hairy guys sticking their
tongue out at me. J-Luv, to my horror, led
his gay clients on. If they asked if he was

gay he'd say, "Of course, you hottie" and
take their pager numbers, though he always
insisted to them, "I don't sleep with customers." Now, I know that wasn't true when it
came to women but as for men, I was never
sure. "Playing this game is good for bigger
tips," he'd say. Sometimes I just wasn't sure
what kind of tips J-Luv meant.

Anyway, I made it out of that circuit
unharmed physically but it really did fuck
with my head. I knew, and know, I don't wanna
screw men. But having all that testosterone
aimed my way was no joke. Energy like that is
a force of nature. I could feel it rolling
over my body. Women at the clubs never quite
hit me the same way. I mean, those gay gigs
disturbed me to my core. Every now and then
I'll be walking down the street and some guy
will stare at me real hard, trying to remember where he knew my face from, but what he'd
really remember was my butt.

With the money Anasette and I made from
stripping, we moved into a one-bedroom on New
York Avenue in Crown Heights. We were both
making nocturnal dollars, so trying to maintain attendance at school got tougher. Morning classes were a nightmare. Afternoon
classes were fine, but writing papers and
preparing presentations became a chore. Now,
unlike Anasette I wasn't stripping every

night, though I was working—by hanging with
either Florence or one of the other women I
met through stripping. Or doing what I really
loved, cutting tracks at a friend's four-
track studio in Bed-Stuy.

I mean, the gigolo thing had always been
a fantasy but my real goal was to be a
singer. I wasn't as good as sad ass R. Kelly—
that nigga's gifted but stupid—but I could
croon as good as that kid 112 and was definitely sexier than Ginuwine or that shorty
D'Angelo. If I had hot tracks there was no
doubt I'd blow up. Back then I was just getting into that game, learning how to work a
mike just as I was figuring out how to handle
a woman.

Meanwhile back at my Crown Heights ranch,
life got hectic. I came home one evening to
find Anasette and Florence fussying on our
stoop. Living with a woman and dealing with
others—even if everybody involved knows it's
an economic thing—is always a problem, and at
that point in my life I didn't have the experience to handle it. Anasette was my girl.
Florence was our meal ticket. Resentment was
gonna build. Shit was bound to happen. No
blows were exchanged but fuses grew short.

For about a year I worked as a mediator.
I kept Florence away from my place and kept
Anasette away from Florence, though her gifts

(and that of my other fans) were all over our
place. J-Luv, who floated between his
mother's house in East Flatbush and that of
various "fans," patted me on the back,
telling me I was "handling my bitches." I
hoped so but had the lingering feeling that
someone was eventually gonna do something
bad. I was as surprised as anyone as to who
it was.

My Vocal Coach Is Gay

My vocal coach is a gay man named Ted. Now, Ted would never say he's gay. After all, he's married to a lovely, chubby Costa Rican woman named Rosie and has a cute kid named Tad who peeks at me while I do my vocal exercises at Ted's apartment in Hell's Kitchen. A really cute kid. It's just that his father has yearnings.

How do I know? For years I've made most of my living by getting paid for being sexy. I can walk into most rooms and figure out who wants to "do" whom pretty fast. I know reckless eyeballing when I feel it, and Ted eyes me, and most men I've seen him come in contact with, with extreme brotherly love.

Lust is a restless child. It sleeps now and then, but most of the time it runs wild. You can lock it in its room but that desire to spring out into the world and rip shit up is always there. Ted embodies that reckless child. His eyes lead him places I'm sure he's gone once or twice. Like I said, it's not just me being vain. I've seen him with other clients: the Latino boy band from Soundview, the cabaret singer from Chelsea who idolizes Bobby Short, the all-American Midwestern square-jawed crooner who practices all Julie Andrews's parts in *The Sound of Music.* He recklessly eyeballs us all.

Ted does have female clients. Waiting outside are Mindy and Cindy, two unfortunately named strawberry blondes from West Virginia who are being patient while I finish up my session.

"Those hicks can wait," Ted tells me. "This is a big night for you, Night. I know how hard it is to get a fair hearing." Ted was rambling on as I worked through the last of my "cool down" exercises.

"Ted," I said, "are you gonna listen to how my voice sounds or not."

"I'm just excited for you, man." The anticipatory look on his face was actually quite sweet.

"Your voice is very strong today, Night. You're ready."

"Yeah. I feel good, Ted."

"Just don't sign anything other than payment forms. You know that?"

"I'm not stupid."

"I know that, Night," he said condescendingly. "But

you're eager, and they can smell that. They're like sharks tasting blood in the water. Your eagerness is the blood." Ted could act like a mother hen, hovering over you, listening to your voice, looking at your crotch. The man kept real close tabs. Maybe I needed a guardian angel, but I didn't really see my closeted vocal coach in that role.

"Yeah, well, Ted, I appreciate the words and I know they were given in love." I gave him a hug, which he seemed to appreciate, and then we walked into the living room, where Mindy and Cindy sat having tea with lemon and honey (the singer's best friend) while watching *Cousin Skeeter* on Nick with Tad. The twins greeted me with a chorus of "Hello, Night" that worked in tight harmony.

"Good lord, ladies, I hear Ted's good work coming through."

"Yeah, Night," Mindy said, "he's kicking our asses."

"All four cheeks," her sister chimed in.

"Well, maybe later I'll see you guys at Lotus."

"Okay," the more enthused Mindy replied, "We get off from the restaurant at twelve-thirty. Meet you there at one."

"More like one-thirty," I said.

"If you need me tonight, use my cell number."

"I'll be all right, Ted. I'm gonna do you proud."

"One day," he said as I was walking out the door. I didn't reply.

My Little Sister Hates Hospitals

My little sister hates hospitals. They remind her of childhood and there's little about those long years Nikki likes to think about. So, as usual, when I found her in the lobby of Bellevue Hospital I could hear a Prince song (today "Raspberry Beret") leaking out of her earphones. That little genius from Minnesota had been Nikki's buffer against the world through two major surgeries, innumerable rehab sessions, and migraines that apparently would never end. With her big, natural, round face, owlish glasses, and girlish bopping to Prince's childlike melody, Nikki looked like an adolescent trying to be oblivious to the world as she stood outside the dean's office. Wordlessly she wrapped her brown-leather-jacket-clad arms around me and rubbed her woolly hair against my chest. I took her hand and we walked toward the elevators.

Nikki had her first migraine when she was five. By the third grade she had trouble concentrating in class and often complained she couldn't read the board. One fall afternoon when Nikki was ten, she was playing double Dutch with a bunch of girls when she just walked away and sat down on our stoop. A moment later she slumped over, cradling her head and wailing like an infant. By the time I'd come downstairs, Nikki's skin was pale as paper. Her forehead sizzled like a region of the sun, and a thick, gooey fluid leaked from the sides of her plump mouth.

It was a few weeks before Christmas when a doctor found a lemon-sized lump sticking out of the back of Nikki's brain. It had been growing and creating pressure in her skull for years. So I spent that Christmas next to a hospital bed, watching my lovely little sister lay in bed with wires attached to her arms and head, and monitors beeping and pulsating as she smiled weakly through sad, dehydrated lips.

Nikki's first surgery had removed the tumor, yet on the real, she never truly recovered. Her already poor balance got worse. She wore thick Coke-bottle glasses that she needed but tried to ditch whenever she could. She was a cute girl but developed a stubborn inferiority complex. And then, five years after the initial brain surgery, Nikki, by now a precocious teen, experienced sudden, painful spasms of pain.

My father didn't criticize Nikki now. Instead he screamed at (and alienated) doctors at clinics and hospitals all over Brooklyn and Manhattan. It got so bad that doctors wouldn't see Nikki if he was around. Had a new tumor popped up? That was the speculation, but nothing was found in the dozens of X rays my little sis endured. After a battery of tests the doctors discovered that the shunt, a thin tube placed inside Nikki to reroute fluids from the damaged area of her brain to her intestines— had snapped and was lost inside her. Twice they opened her up before they found the shunt, wrapped like a noose around her liver. Ever since that discovery, life had been a chore for Nikki, which she lightened with partying, men, and a strange kind of emotional arrested development—one, I guess, not dissimilar to mine.

On Bellevue's third floor we entered the office of Dr. Roshumba Morrison, a walnut-colored, round-faced, sturdy-looking woman of about forty who wore expensive earrings and a nice gold necklace along with her doctor's gown. No wedding ring. I couldn't help it when I locked eyes with her and held her hand a beat too long. Occupational habit.

I waited in the hallway during the examination, sitting

on a plastic chair, fantasizing about standing at a Radio City Music Hall podium and accepting the Grammy for Album of the Year from a jealous, pouting Alicia Keys. I was brought back to reality by the sight of a little Asian boy being wheeled past with an IV in his slender arm.

Dr. Morrison came out and called me into her office. "Nikki is fine," she told us. "Her condition hasn't deteriorated. She just needs to watch the physical activity. Nikki's a strong girl or she would never have survived, but she must monitor herself. She can hang out, party— you know what I mean—but it must be done in moderation."

"Yeah," I said to Nikki, "that marathon training shit is over."

"Night," she said with her trademark giggle, "you need to stop."

The doctor eyed us both a moment and then commented, "You two have a good relationship, I see."

"Today we do," I replied. "Tomorrow she'll be cursing me out."

"No," Nikki said, "I'd never curse my big bro," and then she gave me a big hug.

As we left the office Dr. Morrison handed me her business card, moved a little closer than was professional, and told me, "If you ever have any questions about your sister's treatment or care, let me know."

Nikki frowned as I accepted the card and thanked the doctor. Soon as we got on the elevator, her face got red and she scolded, "Do not fuck my doctor."

"I'm not gonna fuck your doctor."

"I know how you are," she said accusingly.

"She gave me her card and I'm only gonna use it if I need info about you. I would never do anything that would in any way endanger your care, Nikki." She sucked her teeth and exited the elevator. Then she said over her shoulder, "You and these old ass women. You ever gonna get with someone under forty?"

I caught up to her and said, "It would be nice, right?"

"At this rate I'm never gonna have any nieces."

"I'm the one who is amazed I don't have any nieces or nephews." We were outside Bellevue now, side by side. Doctors and patients strolled by. I continued, "The doctor was definitely giving you a heads-up about your behavior. You should be paying attention. I don't wanna have to visit you in a recovery room again."

Nikki didn't show any anger. She just said evenly,

"I'm not doing anything you don't—except, of course, having sex with people who grew up on Motown."

This shut me up for a minute. We loved each other, but we were both living a little too close to the edge, so much so that we really couldn't tell each other shit. We were so close, yet there were a few closed doors between us.

Seizing the moment, Nikki said assertively, "Now lemme ask you a question: You called your father lately?" Another sore point.

"You know I haven't. Anyway, why should I?"

"He asks about you all the time."

"Concern is a wonderful thing, Sis—when it's justified. When I needed that nigga to be concerned, he wasn't. End of story."

"It's not about the past, Night," she said passionately. "You know I have issues with him, too. But life is too long to hate a sick old man. You know that diabetes is kicking his ass."

"Listen, you need some money?"

"You know I do."

"That's right. So walk me to an ATM and don't ask again about that fool. I can't fuck with him. Let's go."

My Father Was a Complicated Man

My father was a complicated man and I
have conflicting, mostly negative feelings
toward him. I will do my best to explain him.
Forgive him? I don't know about that. Before
I was born he was one hell of a man. My rela-
tives say it. Older people tell me. The
clippings in the photo album talk of rallies
and marches. The FBI file he sued for, with
so many words and names crossed out, prove
he'd made some kind of mark.

Back in the late '60s, when Black Power
was that era's hip-hop and "Burn, baby, burn"
rolled from the lips of Afro'd brothers in
berets, my father was an activist who knew
Huey, H. Rap, and others whose favorite
drink was the Molotov cocktail. Out of a
storefront three blocks from where I was
raised he ran SOUL (Soldiers Organized to
Unite and Liberate). From that self-created
platform, my father preached self-defense,
cultural nationalism, and fuck-the-pigs
militancy (not necessarily in that order).
Funded by private donors, foundation grants,
and the sale of handmade dashikis, SOUL got

involved in issues like poor garbage collection, police brutality, and voter registra-
tion. Several pictures in his photo album
show him with a bullhorn, inciting the
community to rise up and kick Whitey's
narrow ass.

In fact, my father met my mother while
holding a bullhorn. She was a schoolteacher,
one of the first wave of black teachers to
enter the educational system back when folks
claimed that "community control" (aka black
and Hispanic instructors and local school
boards) would make inner-city schools better.
It was a time of great optimism, I guess,
though I personally have little recollection
of optimistic black folk. From the photos
I've seen, my parents' wedding was a red,
black, & green affair highlighted by African
drummers, jumping the broom, and much
speechifying.

By the time I was old enough to be conscious of the world, Afros had shrunk, funk
was out, disco was in, and black activism was
getting corny. SOUL's office closed as white
folks stopped donating, dashikis were super-
seded by polyester pants, and my father
needed a real job.

One of his homeys had landed a slave
working for a newly elected Negro congressman. So by going through Democratic channels

my dashiki-wearing, bullhorn-using, community-agitating father became a mailman. Out with revolution—in with civil service. My first memory of the man is not of my father leading a rally but of the man pushing a cart in a blue uni with a Malcolm X tape blaring on his miniature boom box. Even at three it was obvious to me there was something wrong with this picture.

Still, things might have worked out if Ma had lived. She surely would have kept the pieces of this angry black man glued together. I was seven when she had her stroke, and was the sole witness to her last moments on earth. I didn't know what to do. I guess I could have called 911 but I was too busy crying and holding her head and cursing at God to do that. My father wasn't around—he was at some meeting for some new organization that never happened, while our life fell the fuck apart.

As devastating as her death was for my family, it was just one of the many crazy things that started happening all around America in the mid to late '70s. I remember thinking normal got left for dead sometime around 1975. Maybe it was just because my mother was gone, but nothing was quite right again, not in our house, not in the world. Certainly this was true of my father. A dead wife. Two kids. Delivering mail. No SOUL. No power.

At this point I'm sure your instinct is to feel sympathy for him. But me, his Y-chromosome dark-as-the-night offspring, I can't let you go there. You see, I lived with him. "What the fuck is your problem?" is something he'd inquire about once or twice a day. He'd ask that question if I ate too slowly. He'd ask it if the TV was up too loud. If I smiled when I should have frowned. If I danced when I should have scowled. It's a wonder I'm not a nervous wreck since I spent my childhood like a match to his short-ass fuse.

My father lived in a state of perpetual frustration, which I can understand but not forgive. Hadn't I lost my mother? Didn't I need affection from the parent I had left? Instead his recipe for parenting was indifference mixed with hostility blended with a light sprinkling of malice.

By the time I was an adolescent the only bonds that that man and I shared was our love for Nikki (who so resembled Ma it was scary) and for fishing. Out on the pier in Canarsie or on a boat off the tip of Montauk, the preparing of rods, the tying up of bait, and the casting of lines into the water made my father's face soften. We cleaned striped bass

together and then ate our catch just as he
and his father had done years before on
Chesapeake Bay. My grandfather, who died when
I was eight, was a great fisherman who told
tales of conquering sharks during his annual
pilgrimages to the Caribbean. I never made it
down there with Grandpa, but my father told
me of their trips together. At least he
shared that with me.

One late night at the private club
Zofia's, the music critic Dwayne Robinson and
I had a long talk about the role of absent
fathers in shaping a man. Dwayne's father had
abandoned his mother when he was a kid, so
Dwayne both yearned for and resented Mr.
Robinson for much of his life. My father was
with me until I moved in with Anasette at
eighteen. My father was present yet I both
yearned for and resented him, too.

Which evil is greater for a child—
physical or mental absence? After several
shots of tequila we concluded that I was much
worse off. Dwayne could always romanticize
the "What if he came home?" factor and con-
coct a glorious, supportive family life out
of desire. I had no such luxury. The man who
sired me was always around, and his negativ-
ity filled my life. He was so angry at the
white man, and so angry at God, that he
couldn't find a place for love. So my father

yelled at me. Every day. Like the rising sun.

And to this day, when I'm alone, when I'm tired, when my nights are too long and doubts about my profession trouble me, I hear my father say, "Nigger, you ain't shit," and I vow not to believe him.

MY TWO-WAY BUZZED

My two-way buzzed in my leather jacket as I listened to the new Café Del Mar compilation tape of mellow music for stressed-out hipsters. I read a familiar message in the two-way's light-green letters: "Soho Grand. 9:30 P.M. Room 725. Rafi." I went to my reply menu and pushed Yes/OK. Outside the Virgin megastore on Fourteenth Street and Broadway I hailed a cab and headed down to the Soho Grand on West Broadway. The usual envelope awaited me at the front desk.

I used to get so nervous on my way up to appointments, wondering what the client would look like, if it was a police sting, and if I could get it up on demand. But the biggest fear was, and sometimes still is, whether the client is crazy and is going to do a Sharon Stone to me mid-stroke. I remember hearing some "escort expert" on TV freaking folks out about the danger of bringing escorts into their homes. The fool said, "It's so dangerous having these strangers in your space. They could rob or even murder you."

41

The truth is, we—the people who ride through the night to bring pleasure—are the ones most likely to end up dead. Our clients sometimes have people hiding in closets and hidden rooms who may (a) beat your ass, (b) rape you, (c) rob you, or (d) all of the above. My current clientele is relatively safe, but when I was starting out, there was no telling what kind of freak would open the door. Once you stepped off the streets of New York and slipped past one of those doors behind the door, anything and everything went on.

When I step into the living room of a new client, I sweep the place with my eyes for anything strange, like Arnold in *Terminator*. Then I ask for the money, but I never take it in my hand. Leave it on a table or a chair or sofa. If I get busted, I just picked up something that was lying there. There is never a direct exchange. Therefore, no transaction. (Not the best defense, but it gives me something to say, should the worst happen.)

After the cash is tucked away, I call either Raffaella or my driver (whom I only use when I go outside Manhattan or have two appointments back to back). That call is crucial since it tells the client I'm not alone and that people know my location. The next thing to do is get the client naked. Legally speaking, no cop is gonna arrest you with her pussy exposed. Just as important, a naked person is a vulnerable person.

At least the first one or two times I'm with a client, I undress in front of them, confirming the quality of the goods. Once I'm naked, the client tends to fixate on my package and all the wonderful things I'm about to do. Once you and the client have been together a few times, a rhythm is established, and from the time you walk in the door until you leave, you can flow together. Sex is a ritual and it's great to establish those dynamics and then let them play out.

The door to Room 725 was unlocked and there was the faint smell of jasmine in the air. Lucy Masterson stood at the window, gazing out toward the Prudential Building, sipping on an apple martini. Her dense strawberry-blonde hair was pulled back in a bun. She wore a deceptively simple blue-and-white dress worth two months of my rent. She had a womanly figure and a prim way of standing that suggested either good breeding or her desire to have had better genes. Her face was long and drawn, with little color save the thin pink line of gloss across her narrow lips and some blue eyeliner.

Though it was fall, Lucy had on blue open-toed shoes
that suited her long, thin feet. There was clear polish on
her toes.

"I have to be back home by eleven," she said by way
of introduction. I nodded. I tried to say as little as possible unless conversation was necessary. Then I did what
she'd instructed me to do eight months back when I'd
first come into her employ: I grabbed her by her bun
and pulled her over to the living room sofa. I didn't drag
her caveman style, but there was authority in my grip
and a hint of violence in my face—all per her instructions.

For some Caucasian women roughness from a black
man was essential, like a mike to an emcee. I placed
Lucy's head on the arm of the sofa and stretched her
right leg over the side. As usual she wore no panties so I
looked down upon a small Brazilian-bikini-waxed tuft of
graying blond hair. I stripped slowly. Lucy's eyes never
left my groin.

Lucy reached down and touched herself.

"Don't do that," I said firmly. "Do not do that. Only do
what I tell you to do."

On cue she whined, "This isn't fair."

"Give me your left hand." I let Lucy wrap her fingers

around my balls and then slide her hand up to my tip.
Then she turned her soft pink palm in a circular motion.
Our breathing quickened.

"Don't speak," I ordered.

I took the fingers of my left hand and began sliding
them one by one inside Lucy's mouth. Now I took my
left hand from her mouth and let her lips roam freely.
My client had lived her whole life with the misfortune of
a small clitoris and had too many men who hadn't
paid it enough attention. My job was to address that
injustice.

I talked to her: "You are so beautiful, Lucy. You
deserve ecstasy, Lucy. You deserve deep pleasure, Lucy.
You deserve deep passion, Lucy. You deserve all of me."
I used as many variations of "You de-serve" as I could
think of. Whenever her mouth was free, Lucy's reply was
always: "Yes," "Yesss," or "Yessssss."

It pleased me to see Lucy unleashed. From what I
knew of her life, happiness was rare in her privileged
universe. I could solve none of her real problems—had
neither the resources nor skill for all that. But I could
make her come, and so I did. With my hands I made
Lucy's back arch up and her hands shake. Then I took
her long white legs, spread them wider with my palms,

and placed my head between them to double her pleasure.

I would have liked to end the session right then, like
I'd hit a walk-off home run. But the game wasn't over. I
pulled Lucy against my chest and she put her mouth on
my nipples, just where I'd shown her before. I reached
down into my pants pocket, pulled out a green Trojan,
and opened it with my teeth. With that in position, I
went to work as my mind conjured images of every
woman I'd ever truly wanted.

I remembered women who made me feel desire and
lust and straight-up horny. I needed them to come to me.
I rubbed my nipples. I needed them to come to me. I felt
Lucy's tongue and the sides of her mouth. I needed them
to come to me. I felt her hands around me as my fingers
squeezed the space between her ass cheeks. I needed
them to come to me. I thought of that Victoria's Secret
model Beth Ann, a gorgeous, tall goddess with Hershey
chocolate skin. As Lucy's blue veins popped out of the
sudden redness in her neck, I made her into Beth Ann, a
woman I'd always wanted, and covered her whiteness
with Beth Ann's brownness. Now Beth Ann came to me
and I soon came for Lucy.

When that was over, when the condom had been discarded and we'd toweled off, I wrapped Lucy in my arms—long brown arms around a papery thin torso—and I listened. Her youngest daughter was dating a man with no money who may have beaten her. Her oldest daughter's three-year-old had leukemia. Her husband was always in D.C. lobbying for something. And she was sure he was doing a Congressman Condit with someone in the nation's capital. Her ulcer was acting up. There was something wrong with her right knee. I was just getting the updates on things none of the real men in her life cared about (or that they were the cause of). Truth be told, I gave less than a fuck myself. Still, I listened and I nodded and I held her and she seemed, for those moments, as content as she could be (which wasn't very).

By 10:50 P.M. Lucy was in a cab heading home and I was in the shower. Caught my man Stuart Scott on SportsCenter. At midnight I went down to the Soho Grand bar. Raffaella Spinoli sat having a Kir Royale and poking at the keyboard of her BlackBerry. Rafi was as pale and wan as Lucy but ten years younger, with lighter, blonder hair and leather pants.

"You are always so to the minute, Night. I love that about you." Rafi spoke English with a high-pitched Ital-

ian accent that was both adorable and difficult. I sat
next to her and I slid an envelope into her lap. I felt her
shift her legs so that my hand rested, briefly, between
them. "Was it lovely?" she asked.

"It always is."

She smiled indulgently at my lie. "That is so good. I
love that you still feel that way. Not everyone has that
feel you have, Night." Rafi always tried to sound
upbeat, perhaps to undercut the tone of worry that came
more naturally to her. For Rafi, not only could the worse
happen—it was always just a few feet away.

"There is a couple on the East Side who want a skilled
professional later, Night."

"He watches?"

"That's all. He watches. Maybe he'll say something,
too, but that's all."

"You'll page me with the details?"

"Of course, baby. What are you doing now?"

"Got some work to do."

"You're not tired, are you? Not from Mrs. Masterson.
No way, José, she tired you out." Rafi slid her hand over
to my thigh and gave a squeeze and a pat. "I know you
are not tired."

"Page me later, Rafi. I have to go."

Rafi looked at me sideways, squeezing her eyes into little dash marks. "What is your problem, Night? You act like I'm no longer attractive. I don't think so."

I stood up and let the natural roughness fill my voice. "I'm out, Rafi. Page me, okay."

Rafi turned to her BlackBerry but I could feel her anger as I walked away. Too bad, but I had things to do and they didn't include doing her.

I walked a couple of blocks up West Broadway, made a right onto Broome, and walked into the bistro Lucky Strike, where the kitchen stayed open late and a buddy was waiting to do me a solid.

I walked past the tight little DJ area and the bar, which was sprinkled with yuppie couples, and up the steps to the dining area, where late-night diners surveyed the French bistro–style menu. There were lots of attractive, trendy folks in the back, but only one had a close-cropped blond Afro and wore a black cashmere sweater. Her name was Bee Cole and she had great, full lips, prominent cheekbones, and inquisitive brown eyes that made you think of Angela Bassett. But it was all about her smile, which was deep, pungent, and hard.

Bee's smile drew you to her, yet always sent a little chill up my spine. It was probably why I liked her so much.

"You been waiting long?" I asked after kissing both her reddish cheeks.

"No," she replied. "Just sat down. Anyway, we have time. You know how hip-hop works. They say midnight, they mean 2 A.M. and nothing happens until three."

Bee was one of the top music video directors in the biz—if you've seen a gyrating belly button or a rapper spraying champagne on a young woman, Bee was likely behind the camera. Various parts of my anatomy had graced her lens. Sometimes I was the love object in a video for a female diva. Sometimes I was a jive nigga kicked to the curb to prove female empowerment. Sometimes I was the washboard abs in a montage of body parts.

But Bee knew (or least told me she knew) that I could be more than that. Tonight she'd gotten me a shot to prove it.

"You been rehearsing?"

"Saw my vocal coach and got my throat ready. I wanna be right."

"And that's where you're coming from now?"

"No."

Her smile made me quiver. "You've been working," she said. "Can you tell me about it? You know you want to."

Bee loved hearing about my clients. She was like a little girl hearing a bedtime story. She looked positively blissful as I described what I did with and to Lucy Masterson. She was a sucker for sex stories—stories that somehow inspired her videos. I'd heard she had an older man somewhere who'd turned her out, made her a freak, and that she lived to turn out others, just existing to pass on her fever for the funk. I wasn't intimidated by her rep. It's why I'd confided in her about my night work. And that was likely why, of all the tight six-packs in the New York–New Jersey area, she was helping me. We'd had sex, but never alone, never solo. There was always another women around. Fine by me. Maybe we were both afraid of what we'd do one on one.

But what we had was great. Bee didn't need my sex or my attention. She'd somehow become my friend, a friend I could kick back and talk shoptalk with.

"You must have an intense fantasy life," she said after I told her about Lucy. "To get with these dried-up old biddies you must be writing novels up in that dome."

"I gotta do what I gotta do, Bee. Yeah, I fantasize. I

think of women I've slept with. Sometimes I think of you."

She screwed up her face at my flattery and replied, "You should. You've got more out of me than most people. Don't be insulted when I say that, Night. I know what you do and I respect it." I must have looked at her like she was crazy, 'cause then Bee said, "I'm not joking. If you can get to my sweet helpful side, you're damn near a master."

"C'mon Bee, I'm not macking you."

"It's a pimp/ho world, Night," she said. "The roles change but the story never does. Time to go."

We took Bee's two-seat silver Porsche up to Times Square and parked on Seventh Avenue. For a moment we stood in that same lobby where Tupac got jumped, shot, and robbed. Some say that was the first volley in the infamous East Coast–West Coast rap wars. I was thinking about all that rah-rah when the elevator opened out onto the tenth floor, near a battered leather sofa, a soda machine, and a TV where two Afro'd video-game boxers slugged it out. On the sofa were two pint-sized, smoked-out brothers in Rocawear gear and a long-legged sister dipped in denim and chatting on a cell. The uglier of the two game players stood up and smiled at Bee.

"Fuck," he said slowly, "Bee Cole on my turf. I must

be the shit." The speaker was DJ Power, club jock and remix master of the moment who'd laced everyone from Eve to Ashanti in the last six months. His trademark was turning hooky dance pop into hyper-syncopated sexual chocolate. Bee received a lingering hug from Power and then introduced me to him, his cousin Sim, the other Rocawear wearer, and the woman, Trina, who worked at his record company, Powerful Music.

"Bee gave me your tapes, son," Power said as he began his instructions. "You got some chops, kid. All I'm gonna do is guide you where I need you to go." I just nodded like this was no biggie and tried not to look anxious.

DJ Power led me into a studio where a chubby white engineer, who was as Buddha-blessed as the rest of the crew, set me up in front of a mike and handed me some earphones. The producer handed me a sheet of paper with words scrawled on it as a track filled my ears. It was a banging Jeep beat with a pumpin' bass supporting a cute keyboard riff right out of a lullaby. Between the dark bass and happy keys the track was a funky contradiction. My vocal was to be the bridge between them.

"I remember this," I said of the melody. "It's from that old jam 'Black Sex.' " "Black Sex" had been a jam in

the new jack swing era for a one-hit wonder named
Derek Harper.

"Yeah," he replied. "I always liked that shit. So bring
some sex with it, kid."

DJ Power gave me a stick of the tree he'd been burning and I let the smoke fill my lungs. He went into the
control room where the blissed-out engineer, Trina, and
Bee peered at me through a glass window. I took
another hit to kill my nerves.

"Take a first pass at it, son," Power said via intercom.
"Let's see where we are and then we can move forward." I nodded and then the track came on and it hit
me I was about to lace a track that could be on the
radio. So I stopped thinking about it and just focused on
the track. For the next hour and change I blew, not over-
singing, just trying to push out as much feeling as I
could.

It was a beautiful thing, hearing my voice over DJ
Power's beat. It wasn't my record—some grimy-sounding
rapper was flowing on the verses—but I felt strong and
empowered. I was finally doing what I should be doing
and not just doing what I could. DJ Power didn't give me
many instructions. Slow up there. Softer here. Otherwise

it was just about me making four lines and some ad-libs
breathe. Finally DJ Power said, "Okay. I got enough
pieces. We can put this together sweet, son. Come in
and hear yourself."

I'd been cutting tracks in my bedroom, in small basement Brooklyn studios, and in shitty, sub-pro spots in
Manhattan. That's what you did climbing the ladder. I'd
never heard myself coming out of real, top-quality, high-
post speakers, and the experience was overwhelming. I
just closed my eyes, not to feel the music but to keep
from crying. Thankfully I pulled it together and didn't get
outwardly emotional. When I opened my eyes I found
everybody gazing my way. I knew the look well. It was
the reckless eyeballing of people anxious to exploit my
black ass. Not a problem. Not a problem at all.

Bee looked at me with the satisfaction of a woman
whose hunch had turned out right. The engineer and
Sim seemed wary yet impressed, like my skills had overcome their doubts. Trina eyed me more carefully than
when I'd come in, appraising me now as a man/com-
modity. DJ Power was simply on my dick.

"You been working with a production company? You
signed any papers?" The producer peppered me with

questions. His eyes were still red but they also glowed green with greed. "No, man," I said, "I'm a free agent. I make my demos in my home studio. I am definitely looking for a situation, but it has to be right."

"Yo, son," Power said aggressively, "I'm feeling you. We need to parlay. You should come check me out at this after-hours party I play around two-thirty." I told him I'd stop by. Bee was unusually quiet, just standing back and watching our interaction.

Back in her ride we cruised down Broadway with Snoop Dogg's "Lay Low" banging. I was harmonizing with Nate Dogg on the hook like it was a duet. "You don't wanna go home, do you?" she asked.

"I have a stop to make later," I said.

"Good," she said as she dropped a hand on my leg. "I have to meet someone myself. Come with me to Zofia's."

IN THE BASEMENT OF A BROWNSTONE

Zofia's was located in the basement of a brownstone on Gramercy Park. Not everybody knew about it—you had to be a member. And even with your membership, you still needed the monthly entry code e-mailed to you on every first Thursday in order to be granted entry. I'd been a guest many times, usually on the arm of some skeletal white woman of high standing and low morals (which, in my limited experience, went hand in hand). That Bee had a membership surprised me. She seemed a little too R&B for Zofia's, but Bee was never to be underestimated.

Ironically, the spot was just a few blocks from Belle-vue. I thought of my sister and her shaky brain and then tried to forget her. Didn't wanna give in to melancholy. Bee parked around the corner and then took my arm as we strolled over to a red door with a well-shined brass knocker in its center. Bee lifted the handle. There was a digital keypad with buttons underneath. She punched in a code and there was a click and the door cracked open. A fiftyish black man with salt-and-pepper hair, a dark suit, white shirt and tie, a little gold embossed pin with the letter D on it, and a pleasant smile sat on a stool and watched us enter.

"Miss Cole, isn't it?"

"Yes, Clarence. How are you?"

"Always the same, Miss."

He looked at a ledger book on the table next to his stool and made a mark in it. "And what is the gentleman's name?"

"Night," I said. It was a little embarrassing to say that to a man who carried himself with some class. I felt like a street urchin. He smiled professionally and wrote my name down.

"Fine," he said finally. "Have a good time." We walked past Clarence, going to our left down a hallway lit with yellow lights, past a coat check manned by an attractive Eastern European woman, and through heavy red velvet curtains. Down two steps we entered what back-in-da-day must have been a stuffy men's club or perhaps a speakeasy back when the government foolishly tried to lock down alcohol. There was a big fireplace, dark wood floors and furnishings, and yellow lights complemented by candles.

Scattered around the room was an eclectic mix of hip businessmen, *Social Register* types, and a healthy smattering of young Europeans. There was one tall black woman with skin as ebony as a hand-carved onyx statue who sat next to a cigar-smoking Frenchman a head shorter than she. The Frenchman stared at Bee, but he didn't exist for her. Sitting in a corner was one of my old clients, Denise Richardson-Byrd, a gracious yet determined brunette who'd dropped me when she married her third husband. Apparently old habits die hard. Her escort was a handsome but fey-looking white male model type. She took me in with her eyes and smiled nostalgically.

Bee led me to a place by the fire. I sat on the end of a sofa and Bee lounged on the rug, her left arm perched on my right thigh.

"How many women in this room have you slept with?" she asked.

"Two."

"Is that all? Me and who else?"

"The lady with the pretty boy in the corner."

"You really don't discriminate, do you?"

"Sentiment doesn't pay the bills, Bee," I responded. "You know that better than I do. Besides, her second husband was on the board of Morgan Stanley, so the tips were outrageous—both the cash and the stock."

"Night," Bee observed, "you walk in a lot of worlds."

"Look who's talking?"

"It's easier doing that being a black woman. I mean, your presence sometimes must make some people nervous."

"But you know what?" I replied. "Being nervous gets them excited, and excitement gets me paid. Besides, Bee, I'm good at my job."

"I've always loved your modesty," she said. "I think it's your best quality."

Just then, Ivy Greenwich entered the room. Ivy was the last of the old-school Jewish manager types in the music business. His career went back to the '60s, to the days of bell-bottoms, soul brothers, and the curly Jewish Afro he still sported. The man had that hairstyle so long the damn thing had kinda come back in style. I'd read all about him in Dwayne Robinson's book *The Relentless Beat,* and ever since, I'd dreamed that one day he'd manage me.

As always, old Ivy rolled in with beautiful companions: a lanky, big-boned blonde I didn't know, and a slender, elegant black girl whose name I knew too well.

Beth Ann. *Sports Illustrated* swimsuit cover. Victoria's
Secret ad campaign. Bomb ass personal calendar.
Slammin' Web site. It made my heart leap to look at
her.

"Ivy," Bee said, "come over here and kiss me."

"Bee," he replied as walked over to her, "you ain't
looking too cold tonight."

As they bantered I introduced myself to the ladies.
Maura was the blonde's name. She sat down next to me
and gave me a warm, infatuated look. Beth Ann sat
across from me, next to Ivy. I smiled and she did too—a
professional, prim grin that was her way of saying "Back-
da-fuck-up-nigga" without unnecessary loss of breath.
After speaking with Bee, Ivy turned his attention my way.

"Bee tells me you cut a track with DJ Power tonight."

"I laid down some vocals for an R-and-B remix of a
rap record."

"We're celebrating," Bee added.

"How'd it go?" he asked, clearly sizing me up.

"It went well. He seemed to like my voice." My modesty was way too false, so I added, "To be honest, I
blew up the spot like an Arab terrorist." My comment
was in such bad taste it made Ivy laugh. "Well you certainly do sound dangerous, Night."

"If Power worked with you, you must be hot, Night." It was Maura.

"I'll admit I have skills. But if I had a man like Ivy Greenwich down for me, I'd be platinum."

"Well," Ivy said cheerfully, "I do know you have a following. Girls in my office know all your video appearances. Beth Ann was in my office today when one of those Bee directed you in came on."

"The one with Mariah?"

"I believe so," Ivy said. "Right, Beth Ann?"

"Yeah." She replied reluctantly and with zero enthusiasm.

"Oh, I like that video," Maura said brightly. "Oh, yeah. Now I know where I've seen you before. You were really good in that." She looked down toward my groin. "Nice abs."

Beth Ann snorted. "Yeah," she said, "he can really act."

Though Beth Ann was trying to brick me, I still found her reaction amusing. "I hear you, sista. I'm not Denzel but then I don't have to be. My job is to bring pleasure"—then I paused—"with my voice."

"Amen to that," Bee chimed in.

"Okay then," Ivy said, "let me get a room in the back and celebrate this handsome young man's good fortune correctly."

Zofia's had a number of private rooms—candlelight, two sofas, a table in the center, all of bathed yellow, bronze, and brown light reminiscent of Paris that made Beth Ann glow. As the cocaine emerged from Ivy's pockets and the collected noses moved toward it, I stared at her and remembered: dated New York Knicks power forward Bovine Winslow; dated a big fashion photographer named Bernay; had been talking of retiring from modeling; had signed with Ivy for management of her acting career. I'd met her at an album release party for Maxwell.

We'd been introduced and had chatted. Exchanged pager numbers. I paged. No reply at all. Heard through a friend that someone had pulled her coat to my profession and she was, I guess, dismayed. Okay, she was disgusted. Beth Ann was the kind of woman I dreamed of. Beautiful. Tall. Graceful. Brown. Had her own money. And didn't give a damn about me. It made me crazy. Beth Ann didn't sample the coke. Instead she reached inside her purse and pulled out a tab of E.

"You gonna share?" I asked.

"Coke and E don't mix," she said.

"I didn't do the coke," I told her.

"Too bad," she said. "I'm holding on to it for my friends."

My two-way buzzed. It was Rafi. Her message said, "Please meet me at Lotus in a half-hour." It was clear I wasn't getting anywhere with Beth Ann. Ivy and Bee had moved deep into a big money convo and while the blonde was a buxom Amazon, she was with the man I wanted to manage me. That put a giant Hands Off sign across her forehead.

"Excuse me, Bee," I interrupted, "but I'm out. I'm gonna hook up with some people at Lotus."

"Oh," she said, her wheels turning. "Is it business?"

"Something like that."

"Really?" she said a little too loudly, as if she wanted to alert Ivy to the nefarious nature of my game.

"I'll have my driver drop you off," he volunteered. "How's that?"

I was surprised but I rolled with it. "I guess you must already be commissioning me," I told Ivy, which amused him and made me hopeful. I gave out hugs and kisses all around. Beth Ann turned a cold cheek to my lips. I whispered, "See you around," to which she replied, "In what men's room?" That hurt but I brushed it off and headed out. Despite Beth Ann's disdain this had already been a juicy night. I wasn't gonna let her fly stuck-up ass ruin it.

Rolling in a Silver Rolls-Royce

Ivy's Silver Shadow Rolls was waiting outside Zofia's. Darryl, Ivy's wide, bullet-headed black chauffeur-bodyguard, stood by the rear door as I walked up. He had an earpiece in one ear and a sly smile on his lips. I knew Darryl as D. J. Jamalski, a once-promising, now washed-up record producer from the '80s. These days he served as an unofficial talent scout for Ivy, so some ass kissing was in order. As he shook my hand Darryl said, "Mr. Night, I understand we're going to Lotus."

"Yeah, Darryl. I think Ivy's giving me the royal treatment 'cause he may sign me."

"I hope that's true," he said a little too doubtfully and then opened the door for me. I settled into the leather luxury of the backseat like it was my car. Darryl had gotten into the driver's seat when he began speaking into the cell phone earpiece that was dangling by his side.

"Yes, sir," he said crisply and then got out of the car.

"Hey Darryl, has Ivy changed his mind?"

"No, Night. We just have more passengers."

Two beats later Maura and Beth Ann bounded out of Zofia's. They looked like two teenage girls just liberated from dinner with Daddy. Maura hopped in next to me, while Beth Ann took Darryl by surprise and got in the front seat next to him.

"Are we dropping you guys home?" I asked Maura.

"Home? It's only 1 A.M. No, handsome, we're going to Lotus with you."

"How you doing, Beth Ann?" I asked.

"Fine," she said and then engaged Darryl in a conversation about cars that seemed designed to keep me out of it. Maura slid close to me and pulled a handful of E tablets out of her pocketbook. "Why don't you join me, Night." I passed on the offer, but as the car pulled off I realized Maura could serve in another, more useful way.

"Listen, Maura, you're cool as shit," I said, "but you know what?"

"What?"

In a louder than conversational voice, I told her, "You are with Ivy, a very powerful man who I want to help my career. So nothing's jumping off between us."

Maura made a disgusted face. "You really have a high opinion of yourself, Midnight. And I have no idea why. Like I was trying to fuck you." Maura slid away from me. I cut a look at Beth Ann. She was still chatting with Darryl but I knew she was listening.

"Maura, look," I began, "I'm sorry if that was harsh. I can be arrogant and stupid. I mean why fuck with me when a man like Ivy is feeling you?"

"Exactly," she said, looking out the window, her ego smarting. Maura no longer resembled a New York fly girl but a petulant child. Her lips were poked out and her right leg pumped nervously. She tossed her blond hair so much I thought it was a salad. I caught Beth Ann glancing at me in the rearview mirror. There is not a black woman born who doesn't enjoy hearing a black man brush off a white woman, even if they are friends. This strategy wouldn't necessarily get me inside Beth Ann's heart or pants, but it was a check in my plus column.

There was a healthy crowd outside Lotus, which was to be expected. But there was an unusual intensity to the jostling for positioning at the velvet rope. An anxiety flowed through those awaiting entry that you could almost touch.

I was with a supermodel, so the seas parted and the boys at the rope (all of them wearing that same "D" but-

68

ton as Clarence at Zofia's, who also worked for D Security) sped us inside with comp drink tickets in our hands. I'd been in Lotus so often it felt like my living room. Yet inside I felt that same unease as out by the velvet rope. Nothing looked different. Damon Dash and Jay-Z held court in the booth by the DJ. Nicky Hilton and a bevy of trust-fund debutantes sashayed across the room. The collected glittering egos in Lotus resonated as loud as the DJ's mix.

"Ladies, let me buy you both drinks."

"Like we need your money." Maura was still ticked off at me, but I just grinned and asked Beth Ann want she wanted.

"No, Maura," Beth Ann said, "let Night be of some use. He rarely gets to serve women under fifty."

"Okay, Nightmare," Maura said, "Get me a Kir Royale. In fact, get me two of them. Beth Ann, come with me to the ladies' room."

"Same for me, Nightmare," Beth Ann said with a laugh and then followed her friend. Out on the dance floor I saw the twins Cindy and Mindy grinding up with two large men I recognized as the starting cornerbacks for the New York Jets. Wouldn't have to worry about them sweating me tonight.

Out of the crowd a frazzled-looking Rafi rolled up on me. "Where have you been?" she scolded.

"Don't come over here interrogating me," I said. "I'm not having it, okay? Now let's talk business. Where's the show?"

"We can't discuss it here. Come upstairs." Rafi grabbed my hand and pulled me through the bar crowd over to and up a stairway to the lounge level that over-looked the main floor. We settled into a sofa next to a Japanese couple bopping coolly to Ja Rule. Rafi went right into it: "At two-thirty I want you to go to this address." She handed me a cocktail napkin. Written on it was a Park Avenue address and a name. "There'll be a party going on. Real upscale clientele. When you get there you'll perform a dance for the guests."

"I don't dance anymore, Rafi. You know that."

Ignoring me, she continued, "And afterward you'll likely have to have sex of some kind with somebody's wife while the husband watches."

"Rafi, I don't dance anymore."

"The fee is five thousand dollars. Our usual split."

"Rafi, I do not dance anymore. You know I'm beyond that."

"Okay, sixty/forty."

"Is the music too loud so you can't hear me?"

"Sixty-five/thirty-five, your way. That's it, Night."

"Okay," I said, cursing my greed.

"Good," she said and lit a cigarette. "I think this could put us in another league, Night. More exclusive. More money. And of all the men I know, you're the only one I would ever think of giving this chance."

"Stop the hype, Rafi," I ordered. "You already got me. Can I go now?"

"When did you start hating me?" Rafi asked in a pleading voice. "When I taught you how to dress, you didn't hate me. When I introduced you to your first widower, you didn't hate me. When—" I grabbed her arm and squeezed it. "You are hurting me, Night!"

"You're a pimp, Rafi," I hissed, "and I'm one of the studs in your stable. At what point am I supposed to forget that? Soon as I get a record deal you'll never see or hear from me again. I don't hate you, Rafi. You just remind me of all the things in my life I still haven't done." I let go of her skinny ass arm and walked away, as shocked as she was at my sudden anger. I was mean to Maura in the car and cruel (but correct) to Rafi just now. I kind of pitied my Lucy Masterson tonight, despite her wealth.

There was a pattern emerging. I was being a little more hostile than necessary to white women who were, after all, my bread and butter. Perhaps the combination of singing for a big producer, seeing Ivy's interest, and longing for Beth Ann had me feeling too black, too strong. That could be a dangerous emotion. Had to watch that.

Back on the main floor I spotted Beth Ann and Maura surrounded by three tough-looking white men in tight suits with a military bearing. They weren't bouncers but they had the look of men who threw people around for a living. Beth Ann stood beside her blond friend, looking anxious while Maura spoke excitedly to three stone faces. As I walked up I heard Maura coo, "It'll be handled tonight. I assure you of that."

"Hello, ladies," I said. "I'll have those drinks to you in a second."

"Go away," the shortest of the three replied. "They are with us." I recognized that harsh Middle Eastern accent immediately. These dudes were Israeli. They all stared at me with that we-hate-sand-niggas look I'd seen on TV news shows. What were these girls doing with them?

"Is that true, Beth Ann and Maura? You dumping me for these three Frankensteins?"

"He's a friend of ours," Beth Ann explained, which was an immediate emergency smoke signal. So I asked, "Are you two all right?"

The smaller guy, obviously the spokesman for the firm, said in a threatening tone, "They are no concern of yours. Leave us."

"You better do as they say." It was Maura mouthing her first words since I'd come over.

"No way," I said. "I'm not leaving you alone with some tensed-up Israelis."

"How do you know we're Israeli?" the smaller guy demanded.

"The same way I know shit stinks."

Before one of the three stepped to me I threw a right to the short guy's chin that sent him reeling back into the dance floor, toppling Mindy and one of the cornerbacks and causing a general commotion. I was taking a risk that the D Security crew would save me before the Israelis rearranged my dome. The two still standing were quick, strong, and mean. They had me on the ground faster than you can say Mosad. The last thing I remember is a foot heading toward my face.

J-Luv Set Up the Party

J-Luv set up the party that ended my—oh, innocence is too strong a word—but that definitely changed me. Out in the same Jersey town where Whitney and Bobby reside, he had a bachelorette gig and brought me along. The bride was a black Wall Streeter with an Audrey Hepburn frame named Kirky Turner who, judging by the makeup of the crowd, had become culturally white a long time ago. Her sister was a chubby ghetto child who resembled the comedian Monique. Everybody else was very white, very Ivy League, very white pearls, very successful, very soon-to-be-part-of-the-ruling-class via work or marriage.

J-Luv and I worked out a tag team act—sort of *The-Full-Monty*-meets-P-Funk. We dressed as SWAT members. Goggles. Fake Uzis. Menacing black outfits. We came out to the "Theme from *SWAT*." After some militaristic posturing, the CD flipped to "The Humpty Dance." The twenty or so well-groomed ladies went crazy. My pants were filled with twenties. My ears were clogged with female laughter. My sweat dripped on several white-collar women. All was right with my world.

So, because I was feeling good and, maybe, because I wanted this positive attention to be about more than my dick, I began to croon. I had never before mixed singing with dancing, but the crowd was so hyped and the place was so nice, I went for it. Teddy Pendergrass's "Turn Off the Lights" came out of my mouth as I danced around the room turning out lamps.

Kirky and her sister knew the song and started singing along, and for those moments, I wasn't at a party in Jersey but headlining at the Garden, basking in the love raining down from the upper deck.

Later, upstairs in one of the house's many guest bedrooms, J-Luv didn't mention my improv and instead rambled on about the cash, the tips, and the audience.

"I don't usually get such a clear shot at a posse of rich white girls like this," he said. "This is a motherfucking gold mine, Negro." The funny thing was that while J-Luv was excited, I was actually now quite nervous. Hadn't had much experience interacting socially with white people. Aside from dealing with teachers and nurses, most of my contact with white women had been brief and not very good. I had never even had dinner with a

white woman, much less had sex with one. Honestly, my instinct was to throw on my clothes
and hit the road back to the BK.

I just let him babble on about the oppor-
tunities the night presented and excused
myself to go the bathroom. Out in the hall I
could hear the women downstairs yapping and
laughing. Made me think how nice it must be
to have money and know you'll likely have
more. I was relieving myself in a big colo-
nial-style guest bathroom when I heard steps
outside. First I thought it was J-Luv, but
the stride was of a woman in mules. As I was
peeing, the door cracked open.

"Oh," a female voice said with faux
embarrassment. "I didn't know anyone was in
here." It was a chunky, straight-haired
brunette in a sky-blue dress with thick legs,
expensive jewelry, and sleepy eyes. I remembered she'd been quite enthused during "The
Humpty Dance." Now she stood in the doorway
and watched me pee. "I'm sorry," she said,
not sounding it.

Now, it was one thing to make yourself a
sex object for money—it was another to have
some drunk bitch roll up on you like your
privacy meant nothing. I knew I was a beast
from the underclass, out of my natural habi-
tat, and her lust disgusted me. Yet I also
knew that my skin, my body, and a part of my

soul were already on the auction block and
had been since I had started dancing. So with
my pants unzipped and my dick hanging out, I
turned toward her and crossed my arms.

"So," I said slowly, "what's up?"

Gail Ann Dorsey introduced herself and
then closed the door behind her. Ended up
spending the rest of the weekend with her in
a motel off the New Jersey Turnpike. J-Luv
dropped us off there—despite his hopes he'd
gotten no takers—and let me know he'd tell
Anasette I'd landed a solo gig in Philly and
would be back home Sunday night.

Gail Ann wasn't a beauty but she was a
vigorous lover and had a taste for debasement
I'd never experienced before. Late that first
night, after we'd come back from dancing at a
local club, Gail Ann led me into the bathroom, where she stripped naked and then
plopped down into the tub.

"You want me to watch you take a bath?"

"I want you to be my bath."

It took me a minute to figure out what
she wanted. Wasn't quite ready to go to the
bathroom. But two beers later I stood over
the tub ready to go. My problem then was that
I was laughing too hard. I didn't want to
make fun of Gail Ann, but to me this was
crazy. Obviously homegirl had issues, 'cause
then she wanted to get busy again.

"Okay," I said, "but first it's time for a shower."

Sunday night I made it back to Brooklyn tired and ragged but with one of Gail Ann's credit cards, which I'd used to rent the Nissan Altima that got me home. Figured I could handle the fallout with the help of J-Luv's lies, but then I noticed that my key didn't fit the apartment's lock. Reality was about to set in. I banged on the door for about ten minutes before the lady next door stuck her head into the hallway. Said Anasette had changed the locks yesterday and had gone out that afternoon with a woman friend. I called Florence, looking for a place to stay, but she was salty: "You should have stayed in New Jersey."

"New Jersey? What are you talking about?"

"I know about you and that white girl out there. Telling her you didn't like black women anymore."

"Whoa! Who told you that shit!"

"Doesn't matter who said it, it's just that I know. It was one thing for you to live with that girl Anasette, but I am not sharing you with some stringy-haired white bitch. You ain't all that!"

After getting a room at the Marriott Brooklyn downtown, I blew up J-Luv's cell phone, land line, and pager. Three hours later he called my room.

"What's up, Night?"

"Fuck you, nigga! You throwin' mad salt
in my game! Anasette changed the locks. Florence is pissed. You've been brickin' me all
over Brooklyn."

"Can't talk now, Night, but it's not what
it seems."

He was right. It was worse. About an hour
after I hung up with J-Luv there was a knock
at the door. As I walked toward it the door
swung open. A man in a hotel blazer and two
cops swept into the room, threw me to the
floor, and cuffed me.

"What goes on, officers?" I asked, trying
to maintain my poise. The cop with his knee
in my back said, "Grand larceny, forgery,
robbery, fraud. And across state lines to
boot!" As the other cop read me my rights, I
started crying.

D Hunter Stood Over Me

D Hunter stood over me with a glass of cranberry juice in his right hand and a book by Chester Himes in his left. I removed the ice pack from the top of my head.

"Damn," I said, "I am honored to see you, D. I must have caused a real major disturbance." I sat up on the sofa in the rather plush manager's office at Lotus. D shook his head and sat down on the edge of a desk.

"In case you didn't notice, Night, you are a lover, not a fighter," he said.

"I think I did all right D. I took on three Israelis and lived to tell. Arafat should be recruiting me right now."

"That's funny," D said and sipped his cranberry juice. "Now do me a favor and tell me what went down."

D Hunter was the founder and manager of D Security, a concern that had organized many of the club and concert security people in New York with offers of health coverage and reasonable insurance. Plus, the cute little "D" buttons didn't hurt. D wore a small diamond in the center of his button, which he pinned to the lapel of his charcoal suit. D was a big man at six foot three, 230 pounds, and his cocoa face could appear menacing to anyone who didn't look beyond the muscles and the massive head. Always thought he looked like a leaner version of the Mets's first baseman Mo Vaughn.

But D was no bully bouncer with a bat. No, D was an avid reader (he always had a book nearby), a dreamer (how else do you organize club bouncers under your banner?), and actually seemed to get off on helping people. He'd saved my ass so often I viewed him as my personal Mariano Rivera.

After I told D what little I knew of Beth Ann and Maura, he frowned. "Those are three nasty men the ladies were hooked up with."

"How nasty, D?"

"They are part of an E ring that's pumping those tabs like crack rock. Instead of clocking corners, they have a string of cuties retailing around town."

"That's Maura's gig, huh?"

"Yup. And Beth Ann's got herself mixed in it some-how, too."

"What?" I said shocked. "She doesn't need the cash."

"You would be surprised," D replied. "Her modeling

career has peaked. She hasn't found a rich husband.
She's bored."

"Isn't Ivy putting her down acting-wise?"

"Beth Ann knows that Hollywood isn't exactly holding
its breath awaiting the next black model-turned-actress.
Anyway, she's not your problem—you have a more serious one."

"The three Israelis?"

"My staff kept the police out of things and removed
them. But you know those boys hold grudges."

"Never forget, right?"

"I've told my people to ban them from the clubs where
we handle security, but big-time drug dealers have a
way of getting into night clubs."

"So I should watch my back?"

"Judging by your skull, you need to keep a good
motherfucking eye on your top, too."

"I hope it doesn't swell too bad," I said. "I got a job
uptown." D looked at his Rolex and asked, "What? You
doing vampires now?"

"Bloodsuckers always have money, D. You know that
better than me, 'cause you the man who protects their
caskets."

"Who you telling?" he said with a nasty snort. Then

he got real serious. "Okay, Richard Gere, be careful," he said. "Rich folk are real vampires. They are some of the most dangerous people on the planet—they fuck poor people for fun and then ruin your life for sport and damn sure don't look back."

"That's a cheery thought."

"That's the world you and I live in, Night," he replied. "You know I know."

"Word," I said.

"Nigga," he said, opening up *A Rage in Harlem* and gesturing for me to leave, "get your corny gigolo ass out of here."

I Sat in a Downtown Brooklyn Precinct

I sat in a downtown Brooklyn precinct
being processed to be shipped to Central
Booking. The detectives who spoke with me
were not sympathetic.

"So what you're telling me," said Detective Toro, "is that you were with this Gail
Ann Dorsey all weekend at a New Jersey motel
and then she lent you her credit card to get
you a rental car. What ya got in your pants
there, guy—a rocket launcher?"

"No, Detective," I said as politely as I
could. "Gail liked me. She wanted to make
sure I got home safe, that's all."

"Is that why your girlfriend kicked you
out?"

"I don't know."

"Well, someone doesn't think highly of
you, Mr. Stud, 'cause they called the dogs on
you."

"Yeah, I see that."

I was handcuffed to a chair in the
precinct next to Detective Toro's desk. I was
embarrassed—I'd never been arrested before—
but no one in this restroom of ringing phones

and anxious talk paid much attention to me.
Just another black perp in the BK.

"I'll tell you what I think happened,"
the detective continued. "I think you met her
at the engagement party, you seduced her,
drugged her, raped her, took her credit card,
and jetted back to Brooklyn."

"All you need to do is contact her, officer."

"She already contacted us," he said
smugly.

"What do you mean?"

"A woman called 911 to turn you in. She
told us about the car and where you were. She
turned you in."

"Listen, there's no way Gail Ann would
have done that." I spoke with false confidence, 'cause truly I had no idea whether
that woman flipped on me or not. I didn't
really know her. Maybe her boyfriend asked
her where she was and she concocted a lie. It
wouldn't be the first time a white woman had
lied about a brother to protect her pride. I
was suddenly feeling very Emmett Till at that
moment. Besides, I would never have predicted
that Anasette would change the locks on me.
The more women I knew, the less I knew about
them.

Trying to bolster my argument, I added,
"Detective, there's no way she could have

been the one who called. I mean, I didn't
know I was going to the Marriott until just
before I got there."

"That's your story, huh?"

"That's the truth, Detective."

"You should just confess, young man," the
detective said, leaning in toward me. "Get a
plea bargain and avoid getting lost in Rikers
for months while you contest the case and
await a trial date. Admit to using a stolen
credit card and shave a little time off your
incarceration."

I felt a huge lump in my throat. Was this
how it had happened to brothers for years?
The reasonable thing was to plead guilty?
Agree to the lie and have some certainty in
your life. Otherwise, who knows how long
you'll rot in jail. Besides, you still may
lose the case. I was scared and betrayed. I
should have called my father but I was afraid
to let him know I'd been arrested, and my
sister was then too young to be of any help.

Detective Anderson, Toro's partner, had
been on the phone this whole time, talking to
someone. He put the receiver down and called
Toro over. They whispered intensely. Every
now and then they glanced over at me. A hint
of disappointment passed over Toro's face. He
walked back over to me, uncuffed me, and
pulled me up.

"Where am I going?"

"To sleep, if I was you."

The detective led me down a corridor painted institutional green and placed me inside a small empty cell.

"What's going on, Detective?"

"An unexpected sudden development."

"Am I being booked?"

"No," he said with obvious disappointment but quickly added, "Not yet," and then walked away.

I squatted on the edge of a rank-smelling mattress and held my head in my hands. At least I was alone in this cell. No real criminal shared my space. No chance of attack or violence. But I knew this sanctuary was only temporary. I was an innocent young black male now inside the New York City correctional system. My fate was way outta my hands.

I barely slept that night. Fear was all up in me. I'd never been comfortable in tight little spaces and it brought up all kinds of unpleasant memories. I used to sex up this woman who couldn't come unless I put my hand around her neck and choked her lightly as we screwed. I asked her once what was up with that and all she said was, "Childhood is the root of all evil." I had to agree.

Childhood was evil for me. I was too black and my mother died. But even if I had

been as yellow as a lemon with wavy hair and
the soft, smooth features of a soap star, my
childhood would still have been a kind of
hell.

My personal demon was "Cousin" Albert. He
was somehow related to my father. A second
cousin, I believe, spawned from a demon seed.
When I was six or seven and he was twelve or
thirteen, my father got Albert to come over
on weekends to watch me while he worked or
partied. Albert was a pudgy five foot seven
with fat fingers, greasy skin, and brown gums
you could see whenever he spoke.

I'm about to tell what he did to me. I'm
trying to lead up to it, like I've led up to
relating all the other ill stuff in my life—
stuff that I've spoken about so easily. This
is harder. Much harder. Albert used to put me
in bed and act like I was just gonna be able
to sleep. Then he'd spring up out of the dark
and put a pillow over my head, pushing it
down until I could barely breathe. This happened nearly every time he baby-sat. Our
"game" filled me with such fear it got to the
point that I'd sometimes pee on myself as I
anticipated Albert's pillow engulfing me, my
nostrils pumping in vain for air.

Did my "cousin" hold me down and rape me?
I don't know. I'm not sure. I don't remember.
Denial? Probably. Psychological protection? I

88

hope so. Maybe a shrink could unlock the answer, which raises another question: All these years later, do I really need to know?

As I struggled for life under Cousin Albert's arms, my body disappeared. I couldn't feel it. Couldn't even find it. I've read how girls who've been raped black out the event itself, keeping the horrible memories away from their conscious mind. Perhaps I'm like those women. Again, I don't know.

What I can testify to is that my fake cousin was a freak and a sadist, and no one— not one person who was supposed to love me— protected me from Albert. It was my father who put me under Albert's care. Said Albert was all right. Said Albert was someone to look over his little boy—even after I'd cry and explain that I didn't like Albert, that he frightened me.

"Boy," he'd shout, "stop crying like a bitch and act like you got some sense." That was my father. Senior was an activist, a fisherman, and a fool, and not in that order. Cousin Albert told him that sometimes I had to be "disciplined," and Pops thought that sounded fine, "as long as you didn't go crazy on the boy," and Cousin Albert assured him he wouldn't. And that was that.

Anyway, I wish I could be more descriptive but I can't pull up more than fleeting

images of Albert's gleeful face, the darkness
of that pillow, my fear, and my father's dis-
interest. Talking about Albert and my father
in the same sentence is really tough. The
worse part is that while I've somewhat protected myself from my memories of Albert, I
have no barrier between myself and my father.

No person saved me from Cousin Albert. It
was God who finally intervened. The abuse
ended when Albert suddenly had his own con-
cerns. He and six other like-minded youths
used to run through subway cars in what they
called "wolf packs." They'd charge in, fondle
women, intimidate men, and steal whatever
they could. One night on the IRT Albert and
company swooped into a car peopled by two
undercover cops. Soon he was dwelling in the
juvenile correctional system.

Albert didn't get released until he was a
beat-down seventeen-year-old and I'd turned a
feisty thirteen and learned the value of a
switchblade. Albert came out of juvy more
fearful than fierce, bigger in size but less
confident in his heart. He tried to dominate
me one night and I damn near sliced off his
thumb. This was around the time I was learning to appreciate my color. I was beginning
to love myself so, at whatever costs, I
wasn't going out like that ever again.

I put that particular nightmare behind

me, but to this day, even if the details
escape me, I feel Albert's mark. I remember
that no one saved me. We are so alone out
here. Fuck the dumb. That's the truth. You
navigate this world solo. Fake cousin Albert
taught me that.

To this day I don't sleep with pillows.
That night in jail I put the one pillow under
my mattress so I'd have one less thing to
worry about.

I Pushed Open the Door

The cab pulled up in front of a seriously posh Park Avenue apartment building. The money inside was so old it must have been moldy. The doorman, a fortyish Latino man, eyed me suspiciously. I told him I was there to see the Perls and a prissy grin passed his lips. He dialed up. "There's a Mr. Knight here to see you," he said and then listened a moment. "Very well." Then he hung up and looked at his watch. He pressed a button on his desk, and an elevator door in the back of the lobby opened up.

Wordlessly the doorman led me to the elevator and got in with me. I didn't speak. The doors closed. I reached into my pocket and pulled out a fifty, which I slipped into the breast pocket of his blazer. "I wasn't here," I said.

The elevator door opened and he pointed to his left. "End of the hall," he said, not acknowledging my comment or my gift. There was a big, impressive brown door cracked open at the end of the hall. I heard jazz coming from inside—might have been Coltrane. Sounded like a classy party was underway.

I pushed open the door to the Perls' apartment expecting to see rich, pale ass vampires engaged in quiet convo as they awaited their rented black stud. Instead there was no one in the ornate, Victorian-looking foyer, nor the spacious, equally well-appointed living room. The lights were dim and there was evidence of a party—half-filled glasses, full ashtrays, the stale, sticky scent of expensive perfume and cologne. I was standing in the center of the room when a side door opened and a short, balding, brown-haired man around sixty strolled toward me. He wore an expensive blue robe and matching slippers and looked like an extra in a David Lynch flick.

"Night, my name is Nate Perl," he said graciously. Like we were meeting at a cocktail party.

"Nice to be here, sir. Is the party over?"

"No," he said earnestly, "not yet." He pulled an envelope out of his pocket and offered it to me. Usually I would have had him put it on a table, but I violated my rule. Cracked it open, ran my thumb through the bills, and slipped it inside my jacket.

"Mr. Perl, what would you like me to do?"

"My wife and a friend are in that room I just came out of. I want you to dance with my wife, fuck her with your big black cock, and then leave."

"Sounds doable," I said.

"One thing," he added. He leaned over to an antique chair and picked up a mask. "You must wear this." It was a mask with Miles Davis's picture on it. There were holes for my eyes, nose, and mouth, but otherwise it was the late, great trumpeter's face. I put it on and Mr. Perl smiled.

"There'll be a young lady accompanying you in your activities. Just follow her lead. She's been here before. And take off all your clothes." I did as I was told.

The door was made of a fine mahogany wood and had a ruddy gold knob. As I entered, Coltrane's "A Love Supreme" was playing. I saw an older white woman— obviously Mrs. Perl—of round, soft pink skin with dark brown hair atop her head and between her legs. Between her lips was a red ball held in by straps. A leather girdle covered her waist, and she wore shiny black high heels on her feet. She was holding on to the headboard of a queen-size bed and stood with her flabby butt poked out. Beside her, a tall, big-hipped small-breasted, chocolate lady about thirty-five or so stood naked save her white pumps and a matching white paddle in one hand. On her face was a Billie Holiday mask.

"Come here, honey," Billie Holiday said in an awfully fake Southern accent. I walked over to the bed, where Billie Holiday took my penis in her hands for stroking and inspecting. We made very direct eye contact, but no further words were exchanged. This went on a few minutes until I was semi-erect. Then she pulled Mrs. Perl up by her shoulders and turned her to face me.

"Slow dance with her."

Coltrane was not exactly Smokey Robinson, but I took this middle-aged, leather-clad woman in my arms and began grinding. As we moved, Mrs. Perl placed her palm on my butt, gave it a hard squeeze, and moaned. With her head on my chest I surveyed the room and saw Mr. Perl manipulating a digital camera on a tripod. Ordinarily I wouldn't have allowed myself to be taped, but the Miles mask made me comfortable, which was obviously the idea. Felt like I'd walked into the middle of a movie and couldn't figure out the plot.

Billie Holiday came over behind Mrs. Perl and began rubbing her groin into Mrs. Perl's butt. Again she stared into my eyes but didn't make a sound. I wondered who

she was and how this sister ended up the resident dominatrix for a wealthy Park Avenue couple. Billie Holiday
then slowly guided us toward the bed and lay back on
it, pulling Mrs. Perl on top of her and spreading Mrs.
Perl's legs. Figuring it was time I earned my money, I
gave myself a few tugs, slipped on the condom I had
been holding in my right hand, and went to work. Again
I looked past Mrs. Perl into Billie's eyes for inspiration. It
was all going well when I felt a finger probing my asshole.

"What the fuck are you doing?" I said as I turned to
find Mr. Perl behind me with a dildo strapped to his
waist and a surprisingly long red-veined erection underneath.

"I paid for this, Miles."

"No, motherfucker," I told him. "My butt is way off
limits." Mrs. Perl moaned through her ball and I asked
him, "Do you want me to finish her or not?"

"No," he said, looking frustrated. He shoved me
roughly aside and bent over the ladies. Somehow he
guided both his dildo and his penis into both ladies and
then, with a very determined expression on his face,
began pumping away. I was observing this with consid-
erable fascination when Billie Holiday motioned for me

to come over to her. She took me in her hand and tried to slide it through the mask but the Night was too long for that. I wondered if she would take off the mask. No way. She just gripped me with both hands and worked them.

Yeah, this was a strange one. S&M millionaires. Jazz musician masks. Unusual sex. But what was really disturbing was my lack of control. In the sex-for-cash business, control was as important as money. Control is what kept you safe. And I felt unsafe right now, despite Billie Holiday's fine work.

Turned out I was right to feel that way. Mr. Perl was still humping both women when he started using an open hand to smack his wife one way and then the other. While vaguely admiring his physical dexterity, I was also truly shocked. I pulled myself away from Billie Holiday and walked out of the room.

"Where the fuck are you going?" Mr. Perl shouted at my back.

I said, "The hell out of here."

Back in the living room, I began throwing on my clothes. Perl came up behind me with his dildo still strapped on. Billie Holiday stood by the doorway with folded arms.

"You are very unprofessional," he said, a finger wagging in my face. "The customer is always right!" His little face was crimson.

"Listen, Mr. Perl," I replied. "You didn't mention S and M. You didn't mention smacking your wife. And you sure didn't purchase my ass."

"What's the big deal?" he said. "You guys are all gay anyway."

I grabbed Mr. Perl by the throat and leaned in. "Tell you what, Mr. Perl. I'm gonna offer you a rebate." I let him go and he fell to the floor. Billie Holiday, still silent, helped him up. I grabbed a few bills from the envelope and tossed them onto Mr. Perl.

"As President Bush might say, 'Make sure you invest in America.' " I slipped into my shoes and headed for the door.

"Hey," Mr, Perl shouted, "give me back my mask!"

I didn't even realize I still had it on, but hey, fuck him. I kept walking and took Miles with me.

"You're Free"

"You're free."

It was late morning. I must have fallen
asleep around three or four and that sleep
had been fitful. Still, the sound of the cell
opening had startled me. A portly Hispanic
officer with a self-satisfied attitude
motioned for me to come out.

"Where are the detectives?"

He replied, "You really wanna see them?
'Cause if you wanna admit your guilt, I'm
sure they'd come in from home and speak with
you. But if you just wanna leave, let's go."

I stumbled alongside him down the corridor, relieved and afraid. I was happy to be
getting out yet fearful this was a trick and
I was about to be Louima'd in a restroom. But
instead of a broomstick I was shown a pen
with which I signed a form to get my stuff
back. The officer was tight with details, but
from what I could glean, the detectives had
confirmed my story with Gail Ann Dorsey. All
I needed to know was that no charges were
being filed and that I could leave. About
that they were quite right.

So I was back on the streets of Brooklyn. Now what was I gonna do? Anasette had changed the locks, my meal ticket was mad, and J-Luv had, apparently, orchestrated the whole deal. My options were limited, so I headed to Leg's Diamond, the strip club where Anasette worked, hoping to catch her and plead my case. When I arrived, Ramon, the guy who first got me into stripping, told me she'd called in sick. Then he leaned over toward me and whispered something that made me choke him: "I hate to be the one to tell you, but your girl got turned out."

I had him against the wall. "Don't play with me, faggot!" His face got red and his eyes bulged a bit. I loosened my grip but not my gaze.

"It's true," he said hurriedly. "She just went down to Florida with Venus, a dancer here. They've been talking a long time. I guess whatever you did pushed her over." I let Ramon breathe and stared into space.

I had never liked Ramon. He just seemed like one of those sleazy sex-biz folks, the kind who'd fuck you out of both your money and your dignity. Yet he knew more about my personal life than I did. And then, for the second time in my life, Ramon would change my course.

"There's a lady I know who loves good-

looking young men," he said, eyeing me
closely. "She helps them make money and keeps
them out of trouble. Bet you could use someone like her in your life."

"What I need right now," I replied, "is a
place to stay."

"Oh," he said, smiling, "that's no problem."

An hour later I was stretched out on a
rust-colored sofa in the West Village, watching MTV and sipping a Stella. Ramon's one-
bedroom was on the third floor of a prewar
walk-up. It was nicely furnished in earth
tones. There were flowers in vases. A black-
and-white Mapplethorpe print of two muscular,
long-haired white dudes hung over the sofa.

Ramon gave me the keys to his place
because, clearly, he saw himself getting
something out of me. I had let him know I was
not fucking him, nor him me. But when it
comes to sex, hope springs eternal. For the
time being I was just gonna stay on his sofa.
Chillin' in his bed didn't seem smart.

I fell asleep on the sofa. When I woke up
it was dark but I knew immediately I wasn't
alone.

"Ramon!" I shouted and then sat up
quickly. Didn't want that fool to get the
drop on me. There was someone in a chair
across from me. They made a move and a light

came on. At first I thought it was a trans-
vestite—long straight blond hair, long
leather-clad legs, and a ghostly face.

"Hello, my name is Raffaella Maria Spinoli," she said in a very thick Italian
accent.

"How long have you been sitting here?"

"A little while. You looked so peaceful I
didn't want to disturb your beauty sleep."
Her accent was so thick I couldn't tell if
she was being facetious or not. "Ramon told
me about your plight," she continued, "so I
knew you needed rest. American jails are horrible places. There is no civility there, you
know."

Raffaella sat on the chair's edge,
perched like a bird. Her hands were on either
side of her legs with her torso tall and
erect. Her eyes didn't communicate lust so
much as curiosity. She wondered if I was hungry and I was, so she took me over to the
Pink Tea Cup, a soul food spot on Grove
Street, where I devoured pork chops, macaroni
and cheese, and greens as Raffaella quietly
probed my past. It was absolutely a job
interview, but even after I'd finished my
dessert of sweet potato pie, I still didn't
know what the gig entailed.

"Raffaella, I appreciate the meal. But

what do you want? If you got a party you need
danced at, I'm down."

"I can help you, Night, and I want to,"
she began her spiel. "I just need to know if
you're open to experimentation?"

I didn't want to hurt her feelings. Nor
did I want to go back to Ramon's apartment. I
considered my answer and then replied: "I'm
an open-minded guy but I gotta tell ya I do
have limits. Miss, I'll dance for gay men all
night long, but that's it. I'm as straight as
Derek Jeter's bat—just a lot bigger."

"Is that right?" she asked.

"Why don't you be the judge?"

Unlike Gail Ann, Raffaella was a very
conventional woman, so missionary was her
favorite mode of expression. She had a condo
near Lincoln Center with a view of New Jersey
and lots of great-looking antiques. The place
was a lot classier than I had expected, but
then, what does the home of a female pimp
look like?

Raffaella broke her games down to me as
I sipped red wine and she slowly wiped her
sweat off my chest. She employed a small
stable of men, ranging in age from nineteen
to fifty, many of whom served gay men since
that was "the steady money." Still, the
biggest fees came from women who were either

divorced, widowed, or otherwise abandoned.

The gig wasn't necessarily about sex.
Some of her employees, especially the older
ones, were truly escorts, or "walkers," who
provided courtly male companionship. Being
that I was black and young, Raffaella told me
my role would be "both physical and fantasy."

I understood that. Back in the day, my
father and the other heavy nationalists used
to bone hippie chicks and high-society phi-
lanthropists "for the revolution." It was
probably one reason there are so many interracial Lenny Kravitz types walking around
today. Judging by my father, I could see how
much self-justification went on. Forbidden
fruit was forbidden fruit, no matter how
political you made it sound.

These days, interracial sex is no big
deal between people of the same age. But Raffaella was talking about being paid by rich
white women for sex. That was some real down-
low shit. No question about that. Still, in
this business there would be no subtext, no
hidden agendas, no bullshit of any kind.
Couldn't wait to start—just so I could tell
Pops I was gonna win my struggle—my struggle
to get paid.

It would be a minute before I became an
earner, though. First Raffaella had me attend
boot camp. My lessons came from the men who

rolled through Raffaella's West Side apartment. They came to drop off her cut or col-
lect owed money or just look over "the new
meat" aka me. Grant was a salt-and-pepper
Richard Gere type who showed up in upscale
fashion ads when he wasn't doing coke off
men's room urinals. Grant's facade was as
elegant as a white tux. His habits were as
foul as the stench at a Lower East Side fish
market.

Grant taught me that "class" could be
approximated—that it was a way of sitting and
holding a cigarette, not a lifestyle. He'd
sit with me and we'd watch his namesake Cary
and the ancient (to me) films of Sidney
Poitier (whom my father despised), not for
their plot but to watch their bearing and
carriage. We'd stop the film and stand in
front of a mirror, mimicking small gestures
and looks. At first it seemed ridiculous,
but when I put on a suit I could see where
Grant's suggestions made sense.

Teddy Tee aka Theodore Timmons, "a meaty
fist in a velvet glove," as Raffaella called
him, was a huge-shouldered man who resembled
a handsomer Ving Rhames. He made his money as
a fantasy figure (the sanitation man, the
janitor, the doorman) who serviced his female
clients by fulfilling their dream of fucking
the hired help. Teddy Tee was originally an

actor and still went on auditions. To hear
Teddy Tee tell it, he'd have been huge if
only Sam Jackson hadn't stolen his spot.

When he wasn't fantasizing about what
should have been, Teddy Tee preached the
gospel of domination. "Except for the times
they pay you," he said, "you must be in control. They must feel your presence—they need
to fear you as well as desire you—the two
feelings are so close they hug each other at
night."

Teddy Tee was the one who taught me never
to take the cash directly from the client.
"Have them put it on the table, or the bed,
the nightstand, whatever," he advised. "Then
take it and slip it quietly away. You don't
want that moment of awkwardness. Don't remind
them that they're paying for dick. With these
bitches, illusion is everything."

Grant and Teddy Tee were all about pre-
sentation. Raffaella's lessons were about
substance. She taught me not what to say but
why I was saying what I said.

"Compliment," she urged me. "Ask. Listen.
For the women you're dealing with, attention
to detail is important. Watch what she wears,
how she does her hair, how she smells."

We were in bed. I lay on my back, looking up at Rafi as she, propped up on her

arms, gave me the post-graduate course.

"And you have to have themes to your conversation; talk about their values, their
children, and their dreams. Listen to them,
Night, and remember what they say. They need
to be listened to—it's more important than
the sex. When they make suggestions on how
you run your life, particularly on how you
dress, take their advice. When you see them,
wear the cufflinks, tie, or shoes they buy
you. You must honor their taste, Night. If
she wants to define you, let her—at least for
the time you share with her.

"When you make love to them, the first
time will be awkward. They'll be nervous.
They'll find it hard to come. But despite all
that they'll come back if they feel invested
in you. They need to know this beautiful
black man needs them and is, somehow, partly
their creation."

I interrupted her and asked, "Is that how
you feel about me, Raffaella?"

"Of course, my bambino." She climbed atop
me and looked into my eyes. "And always give
them what they need. Always."

At that point in my life I was, if not in
love with Raffaella, at least incredibly
infatuated with her. She found me an apartment. She encouraged my singing. She taught

me how to make love to a woman in ways I'd
never have imagined. It was a beautiful edu-
cation.

And then it was over. There was "new
meat" to be trained. Enrique was a Washington
Heights Dominican, cute as a Menudo member,
and had a rich, smooth tan. And unlike me,
he wasn't against doing men. "I'm about
the paper, bro," he told me one evening at
Raffaella's. It was his choice, but it immediately made him a more valuable piece of
merchandise. He'd fuck whomever he was
told to.

Raffaella told me privately that Enrique
would burn out quickly, whereas I was "a talent for the long haul." Still, watching Rafi
gloat over the commissions she earned off
Enrique irked me. The guy was so eager he
began advertising in the back of _The Village
Voice_, where he'd do (or get done by) anyone
with a cell and $350 (plus tips). And he
didn't burn out. This Enrique was some new-
age sex stud. I did my thing. No doubt about
that. But Enrique became Raffaella's financial touchstone. Over time, my relationship
with Raffaella changed and never got back to
where it began. I'm sure that was for the
best.

THE NEON SIGN OUTSIDE

The neon sign outside advertised a twenty-four-hour diner, a place where pickles sat in jars atop tables and the menus offered cheese blintzes and matzo balls. The furnishings were classic: Formica tables, a shiny, oft-scrubbed counter, shelves of glass-enclosed baked goods, round booths for hungry groups. It was the kind of mid-twentieth-century joint that was rapidly disappearing in the early twenty-first century.

This Hell's Kitchen diner had, quite by accident, become a hipsters' post-party breakfast spot. It was near several large clubs and had authentic retro-cool architecture. A Senegalese party promoter named Alex rolled in one night, scoped out the ambience, and made a proposal to the owners: what about an after-hours club in the basement? Alex had never even been down there, but he guessed correctly that there must be a lot of retro-cool fixtures down below gathering dust. After some remodeling, Alex was in business, and the Cavern was born.

From one to six in the morning, the diner's basement
filled with customers from upstairs, spillover from clubs,
and various low- to mid-level vampires (musicians, jour-
nalists, strippers, stand-up comics, drug dealers) for
whom daylight marked the end of their workday. It was
my destination after the Park Avenue debacle. I needed
a drink, some friendly company, and time to think.
Besides, DJ Power spun there, and I wanted to miss no
ass-kissing opportunity.

It had been a way too eventful night. Singing on
Power's track seemed to have happened years ago.
After that it had all been downhill. My head still hurt
from Lotus. I needed to get a grip, and the Cavern
seemed the right place grab hold. Upstairs, a few familiar faces were chowing down. I said "What's up?" to a
few heads and then went downstairs. I'd only taken
three steps down when I stopped. I heard a strange,
wonderful sound coming up from the Cavern. It was my
voice. My voice singing.

I walked down the steps with a huge grin on my face.
In the back of the room, past the small drink-holding
tables and the small blue stiff-backed chairs and the little
dance floor that was actually crowded at this wee hour, I

saw DJ Power standing, with his arms folded, behind two turntables.

As I walked across the dance floor, I was surrounded by my voice coming from speakers. I felt good. I felt light-headed. I felt like my back was being touched by the right hand of God and his left was massaging my dick.

"Looky here," he said. "Looky here. What's up, star?" DJ Power reached over the turntables and hugged me. "I burned a CD in the studio after the session and brought it with me," he said after he let me go. "I do that some-times when I DJ here, just to see how people react and how the track sounds through a club system. I've been here since two and have played it a couple of times. Look around, Night. People are feeling it."

I glanced behind me at the dance floor, where dancers were grooving like it was Jay-Z's new joint. At the tables, people were absently nodding their heads and feet. Even those who weren't really paying attention to the music moved subliminally to this jam.

"Damn," I said, turning back to him. He pulled a bot-tle of Cristal and a glass from behind the DJ setup.

"Take this," he said, "and enjoy. Someone from my

camp will get at you tomorrow. I wanna hear your demo and get at you real serious."

I took the bottle and the glass and just floated over to an empty table. DJ Power mixed my voice in with Eric Sermon's "Music," and it was like my voice was melting right into that record's Marvin Gaye sample. I pulled the Miles Davis mask out of my jacket and dropped it under the table, like a gum wrapper. Now *this* was what my life was supposed to be about. Chillin' at a club with Criss, and my jam filling the room. All I needed was a dime piece and I'd be set.

Just then Beth Ann sat down. Had I died and gone to heaven?

"Hey," I said quickly, "would you like some champagne?"

"Where do you live?" she replied.

"Down in Alphabet City," I said, then added quickly, "I'm just waiting on my condo in TriBeCa to be finished. I—"

"Okay," she said, cutting me off. "Let's go."

"Let's go where?"

"To your apartment. We need to go now." Beth Ann stood up. So did I.

"Did you hear the song before this? That was me singing. DJ Power put me down on a rap track. I—"

"Tell me in the cab," she said and took me by the hand.

This world-class beauty who a few hours ago thought I was scum, was now leading me to the stairs. DJ Power looked at me with awe as we strode by. My ego believed this was about how Beth Ann had realized that I was a dime piece my damn self.

Unfortunately I'd been around too many women to let my imagination run too wild. Something serious was up and I knew it had to do with those damn Israeli drug dealers. Outside the diner, Beth Ann raised her hand and three cabs materialized out of thin air. We took the cleanest-looking vehicle and I gave the driver my address. Then I looked over at Beth Ann, who immediately began crying.

"All right," I said calmly, "what goes on?"

"I need a place to stay where no one can find me," she said through her tears.

"Are those three guys from Lotus after you?"

"In a way," she said, wiping her eyes. "It's complicated."

"I see," I said. "Is Maura all right?"

"I hope so," she said, and then the tears started again. I reached over to comfort her, but Beth Ann turned away and I retreated to my corner of the back-seat. We were silent the rest of the way downtown.

I hadn't been expecting company. In fact, I rarely brought women to my place. Really almost never. This was my private space—I ate alone, I slept here alone, and I made music alone. Yeah, I had a mirror over my bed, but that was for me to see myself. Some mornings I just needed to know I was there and that I possessed myself. The mirror allowed me to believe that even when life made me doubt it.

When Beth Ann walked in, her still-moist eyes sur-veyed my place with amusement. Don't know what she had expected, but what she got brought a sly smile to her tear-stained face.

"What?" I said awaiting the insult.

"The mirror over the bed."

"You like it?"

"Of course not. It's so tacky. But—" She slumped down on my bed and gazed up at herself. "I do need a place to sleep." Fully clothed and exhausted, Beth Ann curled up at the foot of my bed, looking like a pretty but disturbed little girl. She fell asleep quickly, like any quality vampire, since the night was quietly giving way to day. I sat up at the top of my bed, fucking amazed at her presence in my apartment. Before I could think of anything else, I was out, too.

MY CELL RANG AT NINE

My cell rang at 9 A.M., at 9:15 A.M., at 10 A.M., and at 10:15 A.M. Finally, at 10:30 A.M., I plucked the phone up from the recharger by my bed. A voice asked, "Is this the man called Night?" I didn't recognize the voice but I knew the attitude: intense, inviting, and full of shit. It was the voice of a salesman.

"Yo, this is Night. Who the fuck are you?"

"This is Walter Gibbs, the president of Powerful Music and the man who wants us to make money together. You awake now?"

I gazed up at the mirror and saw a sleep-deprived, ashy version of myself in the mirror. I looked down at the bottom of my bed, where Beth Ann lay curled up, sad, sexy, and asleep. I was alive. But awake? I wasn't sure.

"Power said someone would call."

"Well, my man, my young partner is a man of his word. So when can you come to my office?"

I ran my appointments through my brain and answered, "Around 5 P.M. would be good."

"Make it around five-thirty then," Gibbs replied. "It's 711 Seventh Avenue. Eleventh floor. Bring your demo and dress up a bit. I wanna see what the ladies see in you."

"The ladies?"

"Yeah. Any nigga being dragged away by Beth Ann at 3 A.M. must have something worth selling. Me and you, Night."

I watched Beth Ann and checked my messages. Two were from Gibbs, and the rest were from Raffaella: "What happened last night? Why were you so unprofessional? I'm gonna have to do a make-good with Mr. Perl, and I understand we didn't get the full fee. Your attitude is terrible, Night, and now it's messing with my money. Call me immediately." On my two-way were several equally upset messages from my Italian pimp.

Beth Ann stirred when my cell rang again. I didn't recognize the number but answered anyway. It was a woman's voice. "Is this Mr. Night?"

"Yes, it is."

"I have Ivy Greenwich calling for you. Are you available?"

"For Ivy Greenwich I always have time." Beth Ann's eyes opened when I mentioned his name and she stared at me warily. There was a short pause and I held on anxiously.

"Good morning, Night," he said, his voice warm in my ear. "It was great seeing you last night and I was wondering of you'd be free to join me for a meal later at Man Ray."

"Of course," I said. "I'll be free after eight."

"From what I hear, you're never free," Ivy said and then chuckled at his own joke. I just bit my tongue. "Anyway," he continued, "I'll see you there at eight-thirty."

"You think you can get Beth Ann to join us?" I asked.

Now she sat up on her elbows and glared at me.

"I don't see why not," he said. "See you later, Night."

When I clicked off, Beth Ann started in on me. "What was that about?"

I ignored her question and got out of bed, revealing my favorite blue polka-dot boxers and my not-inconsiderable bulge. Beth Ann inspected the merchandise but kept her edge and seemed genuinely unimpressed. "You didn't tell Ivy I was here, did you?"

I walked over to the fridge and pulled out a carton of OJ. "Were you listening?" I said. "Our conversation, believe it or not, was not about you. It was about me. I think he wants to manage me. What do you think?"

"I don't have any thoughts about it," Beth Ann replied haughtily. She pulled her cell out of her purse and began checking her messages. Her cheeks were streaked with the shadow of last night's tears and her eyes were watery after a very hard sleep. Still she was one fine, ill-tempered specimen of African-American womanhood. A little on the skinny side, but put a couple of babies in her and it all would be Mop & Glo.

There were a lot of messages. She listened to each like her life depended on it. I poured her some OJ and handed the glass to her. Didn't even say "Thank you," but then, I hadn't expected her to.

In the far room of my apartment was my home studio. It was one reason I hadn't moved yet—I'd put all my extra cash into DATs, MIDIs, and various other bits of recording equipment. I'd been waiting for calls like Ivy's and Gibbs's forever. So I burned copies of my three-song demo for them as well as for Power. By the time I'd finished labeling the last of the three CDs, I felt Beth Ann's presence over my shoulder. I turned and said, "Good morning." She was leaning against the door-jamb, holding a copy of *Artforum* in her hand. Looked like she'd been crying again. She returned my greeting in a rare show of civility.

"What are your plans?" I asked.

"I don't know," she said and wasn't lying.

"Go tell Ivy you need help. That's what he does."

"I could do that," she replied but clearly wasn't planning on it.

"Can you tell me what happened after I got kicked around at Lotus?"

Beth Ann sighed and her face wasn't so beautiful. The beginnings of worry lines appeared on her forehead and around her mouth. Her shoulders slumped. She looked downward, like an old lady unsure she could make it up the stairs one more time.

"As you may have noticed," she began, "Maura and I had a lot of E."

To move things along I cut in: "D told me you and Maura were dealing for the Israelis."

She got even more worried. "D told you? When?"

"When I woke up from the greeting from your Middle Eastern friends."

Now she got accusatory again. The old lady was gone. Beth Ann was back. "Why would he tell you?"

I'd had it with Beth Ann and her condescending voice. "Listen, you are in my house hiding from some nasty killa-type motherfuckers, so watch your tone with me."

Beth Ann bit her sharp tongue and then blurted, "But I believe he's involved with them himself. To move in volume you need the security guards not to care. I know you know that. What I don't understand is why D would tell you anything about me?"

I stood up and got in her face. "D is one of the few people in New York I trust. He actually cares about people. Can't see him sanctioning dealing, even if you think so."

Beth Ann's cell rang. She looked down at the number and got seriously frightened.

"What's wrong, Beth Ann? If I can help you, I will." That must have been my dick talking, because it wasn't my brain. Any reasonable man would have tossed her out for nasty attitude alone, much less the mini ass-whipping I'd taken for her ungrateful ass.

"Look," she said slowly, "Maura's been kidnapped by the dealers." I stood there and waited for more. "She owes them money. They think I'm rich but I have my own problems. They think I know all kinds of people and they want me to move a load of E for them or they're gonna hurt Maura. That's it, okay?"

Beth Ann looked downright ugly right then. I said, "You can stay here today if you like. But I have a lot of business to tend to today and I need to start doing it."

I walked past her, toward the bathroom, trying to act calm with the blood rushing to my head.

"Night," she said. I turned toward her. "I know you know a lot of people. Do you know any who sell drugs—I mean really sell drugs? People who could move a large quantity of E?"

I should have said no. Instead I said, "Maybe."

"Can you talk to them, Night? I am in serious trouble and I want as few people to know as possible. I know you know how to keep business quiet. You can help me out and I'll give you a cut."

"I don't want a cut," I said. "I don't want a dime of whatever shit you're into. Just don't let anybody know you stayed here, okay? But what you can do is juice me to Ivy. You help me with him and we'll be even."

"That's not a problem, Night." She walked toward me. "Thank you, Night. Thank you so much." She embraced me and kissed me on the cheek. I didn't relax into it. I just let her take me and then I slid away from her and into my kitchen shower. I closed the glass door behind me, turned on the shower, and closed my eyes. I could sense her glancing at my body through the glass. Could have been a sensual moment, just like in my mind when I made love to Lucy Masterson. But that wasn't what I felt. I was mad worried. I could feel right down to my core that Beth Ann was bad, bad news.

We Stood Before a Wall

We stood before a wall of beautifully framed, skillfully arranged photos of androgenous French junkies. The photographer was famous, the gallery prestigious, and the price tags on these shots were higher than the combined income of a floor of public-housing families. The scrawny Parisian addicts lounged in a posh eighteenth-century drawing room decorated with ornate sofas and thick rugs. The disconnect between the disheveled subjects and their regal surroundings was obviously the photographer's point. Polly Phillips Colewitz mentioned this to me and I said, "Oh, yeah. Of course," like I knew it all along.

Polly was a petite, sharp-featured woman with fluffy brown hair and the saddest dewy gray eyes in the world. I'd met her through Lucy, my Soho Grand Hotel regular. When we were introduced she said, "I like your arms," even though I was wearing a jacket. So whenever we were together she held onto my arms with a loose, clingy grip, sort of like I was a very sporty purse. She was somewhere near seventy.

Polly and I didn't have sex. She said, "I'm through with all that," which was a relief, but when she wanted a man around who wasn't a relative, a doctor, or an anxious old suitor, Polly would give me a call. We'd go to a museum or a gallery, because art was her passion. Which was why Beth Ann found copies of *Artforum* around my apartment. With Polly I was an escort in the truest sense—I was her accompaniment, like a pianist with a singer. Oh, yeah, she paid a fee for my time, but I often got more out of our sessions than she did.

It's strange to acknowledge, but Polly was in some weird way a mother figure. Certainly she was old enough to be my mother, though there was no physical similarity. My mother was a tall, big-boned Southern gal with a loud voice; Polly had lived most of her life as the quiet wife of a diligent businessman who made his fortune putting soap dispensers in Midwestern gas stations. While Mr. Colewitz kept Middle America's steering wheels sanitary, Mrs. Colewitz raised three kids, bought a lot of haute couture clothing, and decorated their winter and summer homes.

After Mr. Colewitz died of pancreatic cancer, Polly drifted for a while and then one day decided to really understand contemporary art—video installations, elephant dung in paintings, and why "real" artists didn't do representational paintings. It was during her initial foray into contemporary art that she met me, at Cipriani's on West Broadway with Lucy.

"Let's try the next gallery," she said, tugging me lightly toward the door. We were in Chelsea, the heartbeat of New York's gallery scene, where Polly and I went in search of pieces for her burgeoning collection. I had become her partner in crime, a sort of surrogate art consultant. Not because I knew a damn thing but because, for some reason, she thought I had good taste. So as not to be ignorant I read *Artforum, The New York Times,* and gallery catalogs to create my own art history primer. I came to appreciate, if not totally understand, Chris Ofili, Tracy Emin, Steve McQueen, and the whole wave of young British artists of the '90s.

At the next gallery, we encountered a most unusual blend of photographs and text by a French woman engaged in a kind of surveillance art. In one piece she worked as a hotel chambermaid and photographed the guest's possessions; in another piece she had herself followed and then had the man following her followed, too.

"My word," Polly remarked, "it's creepy."

"Yeah," I agreed, "but I like it. Makes you wonder, doesn't it?"

"Wonder about being followed?"

"Yeah. Sometimes I feel like I'm being watched. And the weird thing is, sometimes I like that feeling. I sometimes sit up in bed and imagine I'm being profiled in *People* magazine and the reporter is probing into my past. I'm acting nervous in front of the reporter, but really I like it. It's like I can't wait to spill the damn beans."

"And what of your clients' privacy, Night?"

"Oh, no names, Polly," I said reassuringly. "No names. Never any names. I guess I just wanna tell on me and I wanna be famous."

She looked at me and laughed. "You know," she said sagely, "living life on Page Six can't always be fun. My husband and I made a lot of money, lived very well, and never saw our name in thick black type."

"I understand that," I replied, "but I grew up watching E! channel and Ricki Lake. If no one's watching you, I'm not sure you exist."

Polly shook her head and then took my arm. She said, "Let's go have lunch," and so we did.

NELSON GEORGE

After lunch I walked over to the Chelsea Piers to work out but all I could think of was surveillance. I don't know why. Celebrity, surveillance, fame—they were all mixed up together as I bench-pressed and then rode the stationary bike. I knew my meetings that day could change my life and lead me on the road to fun self-revelation.

I was having a protein smoothie in the gym's dining area when Raffaella came out of a yoga studio, spotted me, and came storming over.

"Why do these things?" she blurted out as she stood over me. There was about to be a big Italian temper tantrum in front of a lot of people, so I stood up and plopped her into a seat as quickly as I could. The girl looked so pale she was damn near translucent. Looked like she hadn't slept, and yoga hadn't cooled her out one bit.

"You do not care what happens to me, I know." She spoke quickly and with passion. "But you should care about yourself. The Perls are kinda crazy and they have money. They know lots of people."

"And he treats the help like shit and I wasn't having it."

"He feels you owe him a make-good, Night. He wants you to come back tonight."

"Fuck him and his silly wife and that black bitch who works for them, too. There's no way I'm going back up there."

"Who do you think you are, Night?" she hissed. People were turning to look at us. "You may think you're a star or going to be a star or whatever. But you are none of that. You are just what you are."

"Have the Perls threatened you?" I spoke as quietly as my own rising temper would allow.

"Like you care," she said. "All you had to do was go up there and do your job and there would be no problem. Go back there tonight, Night? Can you do that for me?"

IT WAS A RECORD BUSINESS OFFICE

It was a record business executive's office. Platinum and gold albums on the walls. A dusty MTV music award on a shelf. Photos of big stars in casual moments, nicely framed. A CD burner. SoundScan reports littered the desk. MTV2 played soundlessly on the flat-screen TV. The furniture looked like some assistant had picked it out of a trendy catalog. Expensive woodsy cologne competed with the scent of jasmine incense in the room.

Walter Gibbs sat with his eyes closed, nodding his head. Trina, the long-legged sista from the studio who worked at Powerful Music, sat by the desk with her eyes open, staring at me. We were listening to my neo-soul interpretation of Anita Baker's "Sweet Love," the third track on my demo, and I was incredibly uncomfortable. The track faded. Gibbs opened his eyes. "We can make this work, Night," he said.

"You mean that track?"

"No," Gibbs replied, "I mean the whole thing—the whole thing being you, Night."

"Are you gonna sign me?"

"That's our desire, Night," he said with a smile and then, with sudden seriousness, "but what's your desire? We make hits here. Powerful's track record speaks for itself. Anybody can make a hit record, but a hot artist is about a vision. So who are you and what do you want to accomplish?"

It felt like I'd been waiting my whole life for these questions. "I'm a love man, Mr. Gibbs," I told him. "I want to create records that make girls scream and grown men jealous. I want to be that nigga that other niggas can't stand 'cause their girl talks about me so damn much. Eventually the men will have to give me love, too, 'cause even a hater will have to love my game.

"I think," I continued, "that I can make videos that say all that. I know I can carry that off, with the right people around me. About that I have no doubt. So that's who I am and that's what I want to accomplish. Marvin Gaye. Al Green. Luther Vandross. Keith Sweat. R. Kelly. D'Angelo. Maxwell. Night. That's how it's going down, Mr. Gibbs."

Had I gone too far? Gibbs was taken aback by what I said. I could tell by the way he shifted in his seat. There

was an awkward moment of silence that Trina piped up
to fill.

"That's amazing, Night," she said enthusiastically.
"You have such a clear vision. It's so unusual in singers.
Rappers tend to be very good at self-definition, not
singers."

"I agree," Gibbs said finally. "I agree. But you're
gonna need songs that reflect that attitude, and the right
styling, too." He paused again and then said, "I understand you don't have management."

"Not right now," I said, "but Ivy Greenwich is into
me. I'm having dinner with him tonight."

"Where," Gibbs wondered, "are you meeting him?"

"Man Ray."

"Damn Ivy is always in the place to be." This old-
school '80s expression brought visions of the band Full
Force to mind. It made me remember that Gibbs had
been, along with Russell Simmons, one of the original
hip-hop entrepreneurs. Somewhere along the line Gibbs
had quit the game and went on the DL. DJ Power pulled
him back in as president of Powerful Music, uniting two
generations of rap royalty. I had also heard that Gibbs
had a rep for being rough on young talent until they had
(to use yet another old-school phrase) shown and

proved. Perhaps that's what I'd picked up from him.
Maybe, despite my confidence and chops, Gibbs still
wasn't sure I could show and prove.

"Tell you what," Gibbs said. "I'll look for you and Ivy
at Man Ray later. Maybe I can drag Power out of the studio and we could all parlay." Maybe I'd overreacted.
Maybe Gibbs was actually in all the way.

After the meeting, I had time to kill. No appointments
that night—unless I did that return engagement at the
Perls' for Raffaella. How I hated and loved her—my
teacher, my keeper. I did owe her, but when would my
motherfucking debt be paid?

I walked down Broadway from Powerful's offices and
did something I'd been avoiding all day—called Beth
Ann. The day before at this same time I would have
been thrilled that she'd been chillin' at my crib. Now I
viewed her presence in my life with irritation.

"Night," she asked, "where are you?"

"Walking down Broadway. Where are you?"

"At a friend's house."

"Good."

"Your place."

"You haven't left?"

"Between my cell and my two-way I've been in con-

tact with everyone I needed to be." Then her tone
changed. "You have a very comfortable bed, Night."

"So," I said changing the subject, "what's your plan?"

"I'm still working on it. Did you come up with any
names for me?"

"Today's been busy, Beth Ann."

"I'm coming to dinner with Ivy tonight. You think you'll
have a name for me by then?"

I told her I'd "look into it" and got off the phone.

Around Fifty-fifth Street, by the Big Apple Diner, two
young African men in knockoff Rocawear track suits and
skullcaps stood before two attaché cases filled with
watches. I asked one, "I'm looking for Adebonojo. Can
you help me? It's about business." He surveyed me suspiciously, spoke to his partner in a West African dialect,
and then said, "Try Seventh Avenue by the Stage."

The Stage Deli was a midtown tourist trap two blocks
down from Carnegie Hall. The perfect spot to hawk
imperfect merchandise. Standing in a long white robe
and a matching cap was Adebonojo, a tall, ebony,
round-faced man with a stomach that pushed outward
against his garment like a pregnancy. His teeth, though
yellow, gleamed bright when he saw me. Adebonojo

was like that—two different things at one time. His jovial demeanor camouflaged a hustler's heart. The Nigerian gave me a hug, then pushed me back and held me by my shoulders. "Must be a big wide mess for you to call on me in my place of business, young one," he said.

"It's not that bad," I replied, and for the next twenty minutes, as Adebonojo hawked fake Rolexes and knock-off Gucci sunglasses, I told him of Beth Ann, the Israelis, and the E. With that welcoming smile still in place, Adebonojo observed, "Your model friend does not relate all the information."

"Yeah," I conceded, "that's probably true."

"You know the old Ebo saying, Night?"

"No, I don't."

"Pretty women make for stupid men." I just nodded. What could I say to that? He continued, "Bring her to my office after midnight and let me see her. There's a lot of money in that single-letter drug. Also a lot of foreigners involved with it." Adebonojo had become a (proud) citizen just three months ago, so he savored using the word *foreigner* to describe someone else.

I said, "If it's too dangerous, maybe you shouldn't get involved?"

"Night," he replied, "you know the racist European stereotype that Nigerians are consummate con men, hustlers, and tricksters?"

"I've heard tell of it," I replied and chuckled.

"Remember it tonight," he said. We hugged and then I headed back down toward Times Square.

It's funny about that part of New York. Despite all the lights, cars, and people, I never feel more introspective than when I walk those crowded streets. One day, I thought, all these people would know me. My face would be on a huge poster illuminated by stadium lights. Pedestrians would crane their necks to gaze up at me. My face would appear in their dreams. Dutiful wives would call it up when their husband wanted to screw and their body wanted sleep. My voice would pour out of cars and T-shirt shops, and leak loudly from iPods. My voice would be in the air—my voice was in the wind already. I heard it buzzing through Times Square. Then it struck me: my voice *was* in the air!

It floated out the speakers of a CD player that sat on the cart of a short Dominican who was selling mix tapes next to the Times Square McDonald's. As I walked excitedly over, the seller nodded his head in time to DJ

Power's beat and my floating voice. "That's me singing,"
I announced.

The Hispanic gazed at me dully and replied, unimpressed, "Seven dollars," and looked away, as if that
would brush me off. Seven dollars later I owned a copy
of Power's latest mix tape, which among its twenty cuts
contained "Black Sex" with vocals by Night. I stood in
the middle of the sidewalk with commuters and diners
and theatergoers jostling me and I looked to the sky and
kissed that tape. This was a great night and it wasn't
even eight-thirty.

There Was a Hotel on My Block

There was a hotel on my block in Brooklyn
called the Hamilton and when I was small it
was filled with welfare families. Outside its
vanilla brick walls and five stories, police
cruisers were always parked. So were the nondescript economy cars of sour-faced casework-
ers with their fat file folders. The Hamilton
Hotel featured no room service, no buffets,
and no health spa. The only holiday celebrated there was the first of the month, and
on that day, the festivities rarely lasted
past noon. Then one day the welfare laws
changed and the welfare families, mostly poor
African-Americans and Puerto Ricans, were
replaced with a new, more exotic clientele.

While the welfare people had a patroniz-
ing system that subsidized their desire for
McDonald's Happy Meals, my new African neighbors had only themselves and their guile. The
Africans, primarily Nigerians, piled into the
funky rooms and hallways of the Hamilton,
bringing weird-smelling foods, flowing robes,
and an acquired taste for McDonald's Happy

Meals (I swear Mickey D's is sprinkled with crack).

Most of the black folks on my block resented their new neighbors because they walked and talked and acted "funny." Apparently these Nigerians were too African for African-Americans. My father was different. He reached out to the Hamilton's new residents using all five Swahili words he knew to greet Nigerians who were more amused than offended.

It was through my father that I met Adebonojo. At first he was just one of the many who congregated outside the Hamilton's doors. That changed one afternoon when I was around fifteen when after asking my father's permission, Adebonojo had me accompany him to a government office in downtown Brooklyn. Adebonojo spoke a heavily accented English, and intolerant NYC bureaucrats tended to give him a hard time. For some reason, I didn't have a problem understanding him, so I interpreted for Adebonojo when the accent gap was too wide.

That day Adebonojo signed some papers that allowed him to import and export goods to and from Africa. Next thing I knew, Adebonojo was no longer just one of the men at the Hamilton but the manager of a store at

the same location that once housed SOUL. When
African medallions were hot in the early
'80s, he sold boxloads. When kente was in
vogue in the early '90s, Adebonojo moved that
by the yard, having it sewn into caps, bow
ties, cummerbunds, whatever. Eventually he
imported everything from Nigerian soccer jer-
seys to Korean hair for weaves, and exported
items like knockoff Gucci shades, Rolex
watches, and brand-name leisure wear.

Some of his export items "fell off a
truck," as Adebonojo would say and smile.
Others came from overseas sweatshops or simi-
lar establishments in Queens and the Bronx.
Initially Adebonojo and his crews were kind
of indentured servants, working to pay off
old African debts and the new ones incurred
in coming to America. Once that was done (and
it took a while), Adebonojo organized a cho-
sen few from the Hamilton into a dedicated,
patient sales force.

Adebonojo was unusual in that he managed
to cross the African and African-American
divide. The cultural and language divide
between the new black immigrants and the
descendants of slaves often seemed unbridge-
able. Neither side seemed anxious or even
curious enough to cross over to the other. My
father, and a lot of like-minded people in
mud-cloth dashikis, paid lip service to a

shared sense of "Africanness," but the Nigerians might as well have been Russians for all the brotherhood on our block.

Adebonojo cultivated the Afrocentric-minded natives like my father, though I always suspected the Nigerian was more amused than moved by my father's embrace of the motherland. Still, Adebonojo was way too smart to let it show, and as Adebonojo's accent softened, his game grew stronger and his natural charm flowed through.

During my teenage years, Adebonojo acted like an uncle, giving me little jobs like helping newcomers with their English and opening boxes at his import-export shop, which was amazing since most immigrant businessmen only hired their own. I sometimes wondered if he liked me because I was so dark—you could see Africa in every fiber of my body—but it was never a topic of conversation. Adebonojo didn't waste his breath on mess like that. He was all about stacking chips.

Being around Adebonojo, I watched how he dealt with Koreans, Jews, Italians, and the other ethnic businessmen in the BK by smiling and joking and tabulating numbers without pencil or computer. My Nigerian mentor spoke the language of entrepreneurship, which too few understood. If Adebonojo had two dollars,

thirty cents went toward food, twenty cents
toward entertainment, and fifty cents on
shelter. The remaining dollar got pumped back
into his ventures. If my father had two dollars, he saved thirty cents (but didn't
invest it in anything revenue-generating),
spent a dollar on bills, fifty cents on
entertainment, and lost the remaining pennies
on miscellaneous shit like lottery tickets.
Factor in my sister's ongoing medical treatment, and my father's postal pay never went
very far. My father could never transform his
revolutionary vision into mercenary drive;
Adebonojo came to America to earn and put in
the sweat equity to make things happen.

Adebonojo did share one important trait
with my father: he couldn't stand my adventures in stripping. "That is no job for a
man," he'd tell me, his usual smile evaporat-
ing. There was no space in his morality for
the way I was making money. There was honest
hustling, which he excelled at, and dishon-
est, unmanly hustling, which is how he saw my
night work. After I moved in with Anasette, I
stopped hanging around Adebonojo. I respected
him, but as far as I was concerned, cheddar
was cheddar no matter how you sliced it.

The Words Spoken About Me at the Table

The words spoken about me at the table at Man Ray restaurant made me dizzy, scared, cool, and uneasy. Praise is like that for me—happily uncomfortable. Manager-to-the-stars Ivy Greenwich said, "I think this man is Marvin Gaye's heir." Record man extraordinaire said, "Fuck Maxwell and D'Angelo—this is the guy." Blazin' hot producer DJ Power said, "We'll do for Woman Only concerts like back in the day with Teddy Pendergrass." As we sat at a long table, dining and champagning, I just sat back grinning and enjoying being the man.

But no one at the table knew better than me that words of love are nothing but lies. Body language is more reliable. Only the best can lie with their mouths and their bodies. You can learn more about how a person really feels from an offhand glance than an entire speech. At that overpriced, gaudy Oriental spot, I could feel envy, lust, affection, and greed all aimed my way just like I was dancing at a strip club.

You see, Beth Ann whispered in my ear for much of the dinner. Everybody saw those lips near me, and that anxiousness in her face, and wondered when we'd be making love and what it would look like. How would my blackness look entering her much-photographed, internationally known, candy-sweet, oft-fantasized-about bod? I used to wonder that, too. They wanted to be me. They wanted Beth Ann to say how much she loved them and to breathe heavily into the curves of their ear. Only we two knew it meant nothing. None of them, imaginative men every one, could have conceived that I was being asked when we'd be leaving to sell a Prada bag full of E.

My two-way buzzed. "I am at Bellevue. Major surgery. I need you. Love, Nikki." I sprang up from my chair as if hoisted by cables.

"What's wrong?" a score of voices wondered. I babbled something about a sick friend.

"Meet us at Shine later!" Ivy shouted, and I nodded as I stepped away. I felt a tug at my arm but I kept moving. If Beth Ann wanted to tag along, fine, but I wasn't stopping. My sister was in the hospital.

On Fifteenth Street outside Man Ray, Ivy's driver flagged me down and offered a lift. I hopped in with

Beth Ann at my back. When I said, "Bellevue," Beth Ann grabbed my arm again.

"I thought you were trying to duck out on me," she said, embarrassed. "A friend is sick?"

"Yeah," I replied reluctantly. "My sister is having surgery."

"Oh," she said carelessly, "I didn't know you had a sister. Maybe I shouldn't have come."

"You sound surprised? Like you think your fucking problem is the only thing going on in the city tonight, Beth Ann. I know it's hard to believe, but real life is happening all around you."

"What did I do to deserve that tone, Night?"

It wasn't the fact that Beth Ann looked hurt that made me laugh at her. I'm not cruel like that. It's that she was so uncomprehending of how selfish she was. Beauty's curse is a diminished sensitivity to others. Catered to from childhood, courted since adolescence, and treasured as adults, beautiful people don't always develop their empathic skills like you and I. Well, actually, I'm kinda vain myself (you may have noticed), so I know the type. I didn't laugh in ridicule—I laughed in recognition.

"That's rude, Night."

"Look, I'm sorry."

She whined, "I'm just trying to understand what's going on?"

"I know," I said paternally. "I know."

At Bellevue I knew the routine. I went to the front desk and asked if patient N. Taylor was in surgery. A quick scan of the computer found an N. Taylor who had been admitted about three hours earlier and was in recovery on the third floor. I hopped up into an elevator. Beth Ann was with me and, blissfully, silent.

"I'm looking for Nikki Taylor," I told the nurse, who was sitting reading a copy of E. Lynn Harris's latest tome.

"There is no Nikki Taylor on this floor, far as I know," she said, looking at a computer screen. "There is a Nicholas Taylor here."

Nicholas Taylor? My father. Beth Ann took my arm once more, this time with not a tug but a steadying caress. My sister appeared from around a corner, looking haggard but otherwise physically fine.

"Night, I'm so glad you came," she said and gave me a hug.

"I thought you were under the knife," I replied softly. She stepped back and looked up at me.

"No," she said, a touch embarrassed. "It's Daddy."

Bewilderment gave way to anger. "You got me down here for him?" Beth Ann looked at me like I was crazy. "I was at an important meeting, Nikki. I am on the verge of getting put on. And I dropped all that to come see the only person in the world I care about. I wouldn't be here for him, Nikki, and you know that."

Nikki gathered herself. "He nearly died, Night," she said slowly, stretching out her words for intensity. "His appendix ruptured. At his age, that could have been fatal. I thought his son should be here."

"Why," I wondered bitterly, "would I want to be here for him? Why?"

Beth Ann wanted to jump in. I could feel her yearning to speak, but, truly, it wasn't her place and she knew it.

"Hello," Nikki said, putting off my question, offering a hand to Beth Ann and then introducing herself.

Beth Ann said, "I'm a friend of your brother's. I'm so sorry we've met under such trying circumstances." Beth Ann had been in beauty pageants since she was a child and walking runways since she had braces. Being sentimental and poised at the bat of an eye was no challenge. "How is your father doing?"

"He's doing all right," Nikki said. "The doctors are very optimistic. Thank you for asking."

Now both women looked toward me, as if I was some kind of roach for not expressing more concern. Beth Ann didn't know any better, so I understood her gaze. But Nikki knew better than anyone in the world about my feelings for Mr. Taylor.

Trying to deflect Nikki's judgment, I started asking, "How do you feel? Are you gonna be okay?" etc. I did want to express my concern for her—after all, that's why I was there.

We went down to a lounge that was filled with vending machines, and Nikki told of my father calling, complaining of a high temperature, stomach pain, and general discomfort. She contacted the sexy Dr. Morrison, read off the symptoms, and then the doctor got him admitted to Bellevue. That's where they discovered that this grown ass man was smacked down by a child's ailment.

"Would you just go and look in on him?" My sister's eyes pleaded with me. I was gonna say no, but I could feel Beth Ann's eyes boring into the back of my head.

"He's asleep, isn't he?"

"Yes," Nikki said, "but it would make him happy to know you looked in on him."

"Just tell him I did."

"Come on, Night," my sister said.

Nikki cut Beth Ann a look and the model piped up with, "It would be sweet if you did that, you know."

Against my better judgment I stood in front of the door to his hospital room. With Nikki and Beth Ann at my back, I entered. There were two beds. In the near bed a young white man with a long thick beard, a ponytail, and satanic images tattooed on both arms lay on his side asleep. It made me smile that my father's roommate was a Satan- and Ozzy-worshipping biker dude.

In the next bed lay a lighter, older, shorter, meaner version of me in a white robe with tubes sticking out of his left arm. He'd shrunk since I'd last seen him. His arms looked soft. His face round. His skin appeared to have been drained of melanin. His head sat cocked to one side, his face resting on his graying dreads and a thick pillow tucked under just as he liked it. I felt myself breathing heavily, like that was the only movement I was capable of. I wanted to leave. I'd seen enough.

Yet my feet failed me as if I wanted him to awaken and see me, though of course I didn't. I wanted to go but I didn't move. I just watched my daddy. I slowly realized I was matching my breathing to his. We were in the same rhythm, which scared and surprised me. Then he

149

shifted his body slightly to the right and stirred. Our connection was broken. I felt my body moving and I was out of there.

"Let's go," I said to Beth Ann.

"Will you come back tomorrow?" my sister asked.

"Yeah," I said in reply. "I'll come back and bring you home." I hugged Nikki very deeply. Beth Ann even gave her a hug. In the elevator down Beth Ann said, "She is so sweet, Night. It's amazing you two are related."

I shrugged and then said, "Let's go deal with what you really care about, Beth Ann. Then you won't have to spend any more time around me. Cool?"

The elevator doors opened and we headed out toward the street.

Changing Your Residence in New York

It's strange how changing your residence in New York can change your life. When I lived in Brooklyn I was a just another young black man (albeit better looking than most) getting his swerve on. My world was filled with hustling, scrambling people who were just getting by, day by day, and often many hour by hour. My father, Anasette, Adebonojo, and J-Luv were all different but, like me, just trying to climb up life, brick by brick.

Once Raffaella got me settled into my Manhattan gigolo/model/vide-ho life, I started living (really visiting) the upper floors of life. In the city's clubs, restaurants, and gallery openings, I had my first encounters with truly privileged young people. Not surprisingly, most of my new acquaintances were women.

Through Raffaella I rubbed bellies with the many rich, married, unhappy mature ladies of Manhattan. Our relationships, though primarily based on bullshit, were easy to understand. Nothing in my life had prepared me for hanging with their offspring, the youthful,

drug-ingesting baby vamps who danced around
Manhattan as if the island had been created
just for them. Unlike my old woman Anasette,
who was a fine ass girl, my new playmates
were softer and more pampered, though not
always less vulnerable. They were innocent
about everyday big-city cruelty, but they all
had seemed to possess particularly deep
internal scars.

Obviously they weren't drug free or vir-
ginal. Nor were they above childlike tantrums
or meanness. Yet the way they took life's
possibilities for granted always shocked the
hell out of me. They'd been told "No" before,
but that "No" would be about which private
school they'd attend, not whether there was
money for a Happy Meal.

As much as it tripped me out how much
these girls took for granted, I was just as
amazed how much they didn't see. Be it
Vanessa, the petite raven-haired daughter
of a black securities trader and his Japanese
wife, or Molly, the lanky strawberry-blonde
raised in an East Eighty-seventh Street
brownstone, or Victoria, a buxom lass with
a two-seater Ferrari and a *Sex and the City*
wardrobe, or Janice, a brown babe who spoke
three languages and had never slept with a
brother until Night fell on her, these young
women walked through life oblivious to

things that didn't revolve around them.

We're all more or less self-centered but I'd be walking through Manhattan with these girl-women and shit would be going down—drug deals, fights, accidents, funny clothes, strange people, new places—and they wouldn't notice a thing if they were caught up talking about Daddy, Mommy, the bitch from last night's party whom they couldn't stand, or what they were buying (or wanted purchased for them). Out in Brooklyn you surveyed the streets when you walked them. You watched where people were around you, who was on the block you were coming toward, and who was behind you. I got mad if a friend rolled up on me and I hadn't seen them coming. Vigilance was better than the Club when it came to safety.

Yet butta-soft beauties strolled through New York like the streets couldn't hurt them. Even during Giuliani time that seemed a silly way to me. Yet they did move around that unaware, which I found charmingly arrogant. Whether they were white, black, or had tossed-salad bloodlines, these girls fascinated me.

It was Tandi Lincoln who touched me much deeper, with her honey-dipped complexion, curly brown locks, and a full mouth that specialized in fleeting smiles. I say "fleeting"

because melancholy was Tandi's preferred
state, and a distracted frown usually shaped
that luscious mouth. But if you made Tandi
smile, her transition to happiness was like
the sun emerging from clouds. The truth is, I
didn't ever really understand her, but back
then I didn't know that mattered.

I met her outside the Coffee Shop, the
Brazilian spot on Union Square with a great
sidewalk café section that was great for hip-
ster people-watchers. Tandi was waiting by
the curb on Sixteenth Street for a table to
open up and I was walking by, on the way back
to my place from a "client." It was one of
those warm, amazingly bright spring days when
New Yorkers rip off their clothes after a
winter of heavy gear and happily rediscover
the contours of each other's bodies. It's a
time of sexual rebirth and Tandi was already
blooming in black platform sandals, a yellow
skirt, a halter top, rose-tinted shades, and
a smooth, exposed brown belly.

Tandi cocked her head slightly when she
spotted me spotting her. I didn't give her a
brazen gigolo vibe. In fact, her attention
made me feel embarrassed. I think I even
blushed. I'd gone half a block down before I
stopped in front of the NYU dorm and turned
around. By the time I'd walked back to the
Coffee Shop, Tandi was sitting alone at a

table near the railing that separated the restaurant from the sidewalk. I came up beside her and leaned my hands against the railing.

I smiled and said, "Hello, my name is Night and I was hoping that I could talk to you."

"Knight?" she replied. "You did not say your name was Knight. Is that Knight as in the Round Table?"

"No," I told her. "Night as in the opposite of day, as in stars and the moon, as in sleep and bed."

"Your mother named you Night?"

"No," I said and leaned in a bit closer to her. "A black mother would never name a son Night. Tarese or Keyshawn or Shakim, yes. But Night, no. That was a name I chose for myself." She chuckled and there was that awkward moment after laughter when the conversation has to take a new direction or die. So I went for it.

"Look," I said, "I saw you standing there and I thought you were beautiful and I thought, well, let me see if she'll let me get to know her. So I came back. What's your name?"

"Tandi," she told me. "Not as interesting as Night, unfortunately." She offered her hand, which was as soft as bubble bath. I

held onto it as I asked, "Can I join you for
lunch?"

"I might be waiting on my boyfriend," she
said, though she let me continue to hold her
hand.

"I'll take my chances," I replied and
then stepped over the railing, into Tandi's
life and one enchanted summer. We were just
two good-looking young people powered by
infatuation and lust into a little sumpthin'
sumpthin'. But at that time, it seemed like
my life was taking a leap forward and that
after all the butta-soft girls I'd encountered before, Tandi was the real thang.

Maybe I just got drunk off my first Hamptons summer. Tandi and a crew of her bright,
bouncy, well-groomed private-school peers had
a share in East Hampton and I was Tandi's
tagalong friend. There were five bedrooms,
five girls, and as a result of that math, at
least ten to fifteen dudes rolling through
each weekend. Fridays I'd pile into someone's
SUV or take the jitney out of the Apple into
a barely post-collegiate world of parties,
the beach, and wealth.

Tandi often doted on me. She'd always
comment on how beautiful I was, comparing me
favorably to Michael Jordan and Tyson Beckford, touching my hair, and telling me how
fine I was. She even praised my cooking,

since, perhaps to compensate for being money-challenged, I often made breakfast for the entire late-awakening crowd. We certainly made a cute couple—the chocolate-brown-dreaded brother and the boho BAP.

But there was another side to that summer. Tandi tended to make me more an object for inspection than a member of the crew. When the talked turned to growing up, Tandi lightly teased me about not knowing anything about Dalton or Vassar or any other school except by reputation. I hadn't learned to ride a horse or played lacrosse or surfed or summered in Europe or otherwise experienced their leisure world. No one pointed at me and announced, "Oooh, we have a poor kid among us." But Tandi, though she obviously enjoyed me, did it at a bit of a remove.

Despite that undercurrent of anxiety between us, things didn't fall apart between Tandi and me until one August day at a Hamptons polo match. Wearing my best Jay Gatsby white suit (yeah, D gave me Fitzgerald's book and I peeped it) and a pale pink shirt (a gift from Tandi), I attended the East Hampton polo matches as part of a charity event sponsored by Piaget watches for the Rush Philanthrophic Arts Foundation. That meant there were more black folks than usual, which gave me a bit of a comfort zone, though these were mostly Sag Harbor–Wall Street types.

Turned out Mrs. Lincoln, Tandi's well-preserved, imposing mother, had purchased tickets and was there to enjoy the day and, to a lesser degree, to assess me. I could tell when we met that Mrs. Lincoln was surprised at how dark I was, though she smiled winningly through the look in her eyes. I could read that look like a damn book. She followed up by probing me about my mother (deceased), my father (a devoted civil servant), and my dreams (R&B stardom) while outwardly withholding judgment. Tandi's mother had the same melancholy air as her daughter, but unlike Tandi I couldn't make her laugh.

Still, I believe I could have continued to be in Tandi's life if Mrs. Jacobson hadn't shown up. I'd met her through Raffaella at a reception at Larry Gagosian's East Side gallery. Mrs. Jacobson was rich, divorced, and as bitter as any client I'd encountered. I visited her at her home in the guise of personal trainer, but she seemed more embarrassed than lustful. That was our only session.

When Mrs. Jacobson showed up, in a big straw hat and Jackie O. shades, she hugged Mrs. Lincoln and then looked at me with an indiscreet gaze. Neither of us could put our

finger on where we'd met. I think I realized
where we'd met first and tried to stay away
from her. But then, how many young black men
with dreads had previously serviced Mrs.
Jacobson's pussy? Soon she put it together.
I felt her eyes on the side of my face. I
turned and smiled. She didn't. She just
sipped some champagne and dropped her gaze.

I've experienced often the feeling of
what D calls "impending doom" in my life, a
consequence of being poor, black, and power-
less in a country where, despite all the talk
of multiculti this and multiracial that, to
be white and rich is damn helpful. Nothing
bad happened that day. In fact, that night
Tandi, I, and the whole house drove over to
the now-infamous Conscience Point for drugs,
music, and foreplay.

But dark deeds always find the light.
There are no secrets in this life. There are
only secrets for now. Labor Day came and the
Hamptons season ended. By mid-September it
became hard to reach Tandi. Messages were
left and none returned. Much as with J-Luv
and Anasette, I never did find out exactly
what words had been uttered to destroy my
character. Tandi sure never told me. When I
finally caught her on the phone, she was eva-
sive: "Busy taking classes." "I'm on the
other line." "We'll get together later."

I didn't see her again until October, when I caught her in the back room at Lotus, squeezed into a booth with two trust-fund cuties. Tandi tried to ignore me but I wasn't having it. Finally she got up and we walked over to the bar.

"Did I hurt you?" I asked. "Did I disrespect you?" She said no. "Then why are you dissing me like this?"

"Look," she sighed, "it's just over, Night. We had a nice summer. But I've got to get serious and I can't with you. So just stop calling me. Okay? Good-bye."

That was the end for me and the melancholy girl. I still hover around girls like Tandi. I mean, New York stinks of them. But now I know to keep my distance. I keep my heart, if not my hands, to myself.

The First Thing Beth Ann Said

The first thing Beth Ann said in the taxi was, "It'll work itself out, Night."

"What?" I sounded like a petulant adolescent. "I know he'll be all right. It's only his appendix."

"No, not just his illness. Everything. Your anger at him and all that hostility. It'll work itself out."

As the taxi zoomed up the West Side Highway toward Harlem, I turned away from Beth Ann, uncomfortable with her concern.

"My father and I didn't speak for years after he left my mother," she said flatly. "I was so angry at him. Just so angry. Then one day I just broke down—I still don't know what made me do it—but I did and went to see him. You know what I saw? Just an old lonely black man who'd made a mistake he couldn't fix. I had to fix things for him. I did it by paying attention to him. He didn't get any smarter or cooler or nicer because I forgave him. He was still who he was. You need to see your father as a human being and not the monster you created. You do that and everything in your life will be easier."

I couldn't believe this was coming from Beth Ann. I was stunned and touched that she had revealed so much about herself.

"Thank you," I said. I felt like an asshole for the way I had treated her at the hospital. So now I asked, "Are you really ready to do this?"

"No," she said, "but I have to be. Maura is my best friend. I've known her since I came to New York when I was sixteen. She's been there for me so many times, so I have to be there for her. I know this is incredibly stupid. I know this could ruin me. But I don't have any other choice. Those men will hurt her and I can't let that happen." Beth Ann didn't seem quite so spoiled or manipulative in the back of that taxi. She seemed like a damn good friend.

Since leaving the Hamilton Hotel, Adebonojo had expanded his operation so that he had import-export spots in Harlem, Brooklyn, the Bronx, and Queens, each employing a new set of Nigerian immigrants. His home base was now on 116th Street, a once-dangerous drug supermarket that now boasted scores of African

shops and eateries. It was like a strip of Harlem had
been transferred into an uptown African market with
Adebonojo's office the biggest stall.

It was near midnight and lights burned bright inside
Call Home Africa, where a bank of phones, a stack of
phone cards, and a bored middle-aged woman sat
behind a cash register serving the needs of Africans
who were trying to reach out and touch the motherland.
A group of French-speaking Africans stood around one
phone. An older woman in the group was crying, while
a young man yelled into the receiver.

Past the cashier, stacked boxes of TVs and CD players, haphazard piles of fabric, and videotapes of West
African exploitation films was Adebonojo's office. The
dimly lit room had maps of the United States and West
Africa on the walls alongside photos of Bob Marley,
Fela, and George W. Bush. Adebonojo sat behind a
worn mahogany desk and was wearing the elegant
white-and-green warm-up suit of the Super Eagles, Nige-
ria's national soccer team.

After I introduced them, Adebonojo announced, "It is
rare we have a true queen in this office." His yellow
teeth glimmered as he smiled warmly. "I have to have

some commemoration. I hope it is all right?" He pro-
duced a glossy photo of Beth Ann from his desk and had
her sign it.

"Oh, please," she said, giving as good as she got,
"everyone enjoys being appreciated." This patter went
on for a minute until I cut in.

"I'm pleased you two are vibing so well, but perhaps
it's time we got down to business."

"Surely you are right, Night," Adebonojo replied.
"So, my queen, I understand you need some help with
distribution."

"Yes," she said. Her beauty-pageant face twisted to
a frown and she unconsciously slumped forward in
her chair. "A good friend of mine made promises she
couldn't keep and got into trouble with her partners."

"Israelis, I understand?"

"Yes," Beth Ann admitted. "She is being detained
until I can come up with money she owes for selling a
large quantity of drugs."

"Why are you doing this?" he asked. "Couldn't your
friend give back the merchandise? This E is a very popu-
lar commodity these days."

"If I wasn't a celebrity, they might have done that,"

she answered. "But they figured I knew lots of people I could sell the E to."

"Since that is true, why did you enlist our mutual friend Night?

Beth Ann sighed and looked down, then back at Adebonojo. "No disrespect to Night," she began, "but he turned up when I wasn't sure what to do. I thought he might know someone—someone like you. I didn't want any people I know from the fashion world to think I was selling drugs. I'm at a turning point in my life, Mr. Adebonojo. I'm trying not to be a model—I want to act, host TV programs, really expand my brand—and being associated with drug dealing could derail all that. Everyone knows Night is a hustler, so—"

Adebonojo chuckled and then interrupted her. "So luck and a little clear thinking brings you to me?"

"Yes," she said. "Now you know the situation. Can you help me?"

"I can," he told her. "But only a little, miss. You should know that by moving this merchandise, your problems don't end."

Beth Ann slumped further in her seat. "If you mean they still may not let Maura go or that she might already be dead or hurt, I've thought of that."

"And," Adebonojo said in a grandfatherly voice, "you should be aware that once you do this, they can blackmail you anytime in the future."

Beth Ann was now so deep into the chair it looked like her shoulders had disappeared. "I just know," she said with emotion, "that I can't let Maura down."

Adebonojo considered her answer and then asked, "Do you have the merchandise with you?"

Beth Ann carried a cute Prada bag that she slid off and unzipped. Out came three Ziploc bags containing blue tablets with little smiley faces on them. Adebonojo opened all three bags and took out a pill from each. "I'll be right back," he said and left the room.

"I still think we should call D," I said.

"No. I don't want him to know about Maura or the drugs or any of this. I believe he or some of his people are involved with this."

"That's bullshit, Beth Ann. I know D real well, and he would never be involved in kidnapping for drug dealers, and there's no way he'd let someone he cared about be threatened. He just wouldn't be part of that."

"It's none of his business, Night," she said with some heat, "and after this, it will be none of yours."

Now I got heated, too. I defended D some more and questioned her judgment. Our voices were loud when Adebonojo walked back in.

"Excuse me," he said firmly, "there are people phoning home outside." In his hand was a brown paper bag, which he gave to Beth Ann.

"This is a down payment on our sale of the merchandise." Beth Ann opened the bag, pulled out three stacks of bills, and counted as Adebonojo and I watched. When Beth Ann was finished, he told her, "I expect to give you back about five times that."

"I need it by the end of the week," she said quickly.

"Well, it may only be three times that amount. I hope that's adequate to solve the situation."

"If it's what you can do," she said, "do it. It beats a blank." Then she stuffed the bills back in her bag.

I looked at my old mentor and said, "Between phone cards and kente, you're doing well."

"People need fabric and they need to talk to family," he said with a bemused smile.

"So," she said cutting in, "when do we meet on Friday?"

"I'll call Night and let him know," he said.

"What about you calling me?" she suggested.

"No, I will call Night. He is my buffer between you and me. I think it is better he stay in that role."

Beth Ann didn't like that but said, "Fine." Then we all stood up. Looked like she wanted to say something else. Instead she walked over to Adebonojo and gave him a hug. Her eyes watered up and she fought back tears. Adebonojo and I were both taken aback. This woman's mood was flipping back and forth like a radio tuner.

"Don't worry," he said comfortingly, "we won't let down one of our African queens." Then he added, "You have a good friend here, Beth Ann. I would not do this for anyone but him."

She glanced at me, said "I know," and walked out of the room. Adebonojo whispered to me, "I don't completely trust her. She doesn't tell us everything, but I do believe her heart is good. She's not lying in order to fool us. She's lying 'cause the truth hurts."

"Yeah," I agreed, "her heart is all right. It's her mouth that's the problem." I hugged Adebonojo and then followed her out.

We didn't say much when we first got in the gypsy cab Adebonojo had arranged for our ride downtown. In one night we'd celebrated, argued, shared family intimacies, and argued some more. What more was there to say? From 116th down to Forty-second Street we just gazed out the window. Then, around Times Square, an old movie memory surfaced.

"You got me in a *Mona Lisa*, didn't you?"

"What?"

"That movie *Mona Lisa*. That actor Bob Hoskins gets caught up with this fly black hooker who tells him she needs help finding a little blond stunt who's drugged out. Turns out it wasn't about friendship but some lesbian love shit. I'm beginning to think I'm Bob Hoskins and you're the fly black chick and Maura is the stunt. Is Maura your squeeze? It's all right by me—I just wanna know."

"Please, Night," she said, really pissed. "Everything in your world may be about sex, but not in mine."

"You're holding back, Beth Ann. That's all there is to it. I'm helping you, my friends are helping you, and we're walking into something with one eye closed. Kick some game to me or I'm gonna pull Adebonojo out."

Beth Ann sighed, looked out the window, glanced up to see if the driver was listening—he was on a cell speaking in Hindi—and then she turned back to me.

"I'm in a little deeper than I said."

"No need to stop."

"I owe them. Not Maura. I was never very good with money and so I was spending as much as I earned. You know, those modeling agencies hold your money as long as they can, collecting interest for their accounts while the girls get caught short on cash. I wanted to get ahead of myself for a change. Maura's the kind of girl who has two sides to her phone book—the light side and the dark side. Sometimes she brings the two sides together.

"So everything went well for a while. Then I bought this red Porsche. Then I crashed the red Porsche in East Hampton. The night before the crash, I gave away bags full of E at Conscience Point. Suddenly I owed the car people, the insurance company wasn't feeling sympathetic toward me, the man whose house I crashed into sued me, and those fucking Israelis got upset. Maura vouched for me and I fucked up."

"Now she's fucked up."

"They might sell her to some Arab oil sheik. It sounds crazy but those boys don't play. Anyway, that's it. You still feel like Bob Hoskins?"

"You don't really think D's involved, do you?"

Beth Ann rolled her eyes like this topic wasn't worth

her time. "Look, it's a long story. It's like a book all its own." She put her hand on mine and squeezed. "It's going to work out, all right? Let's just keep it on the DL together and we can make it all go away." She leaned over and kissed me. It wasn't a passionate kiss but a probing one. She wanted to see how I'd react and I just wanted to feel my tongue in her mouth. I didn't embrace her—but I didn't push her away. I just lingered in the space between lust and relaxation and let her pull away and slide back over to her side.

"You still don't trust me, do you?"

"If you want to kiss me after this is over, I'll want to kiss you, too. But remember what I do for a living. Sex and money go hand in hand. When they separate in a few days, let's see where we're at. How's that sound?"

"Like a businessman," she said. "Like a business-man." She studied me a moment and then suggested, "You should go meet Ivy and Gibbs, you know."

"Not the way I feel," I replied. "Let them think we're somewhere getting busy. That's actually better for them to think right now. You make me larger in their horny old eyes."

"Little do they know," she said.

"True dat," I replied with hip-hop inflection. My two-way buzzed. Raffaella again. "IT'S NOT TOO LATE TO HELP ME."

I wrote back, "I'm going home," and sent it off.

"You're going home?" I asked Beth Ann.

"No. I need to make a stop," she said. "I'm gonna try to get this money to the Israelis and see about Maura."

"You need me to come with you?"

"Yes, but no. They are scary, but they'll remember you and it could get ugly. I'll be fine. Let me off at Hush."

Hush was a disco/lounge off Fifth Avenue in the Flat-iron District. A nice enough spot, but normally passé for a hot gal like Beth Ann. When the taxi stopped in front, there was a real awkward moment. Wasn't sure if we should hug, kiss, or punch each other out. Beth Ann opted for a hug and a kiss on the cheek.

"Call me tomorrow," I said. "Let me know what goes on. Adebonojo is a great man. He may steal a bit but he won't rip you off."

"I could feel that," she said. And then Beth Ann was gone and off into Hush. My soul told me to stay and be a protector but my mind was more persuasive.

I Don't Have Many Close Friends

I don't have many close friends. Maybe
it's because of my childhood. Perhaps my
night work has made me too secretive and
guarded. Whatever the reason, not too many
people get near my Virgo soul. In their own
way, Raffaella and D were probably my best
friends—a pimp and a security guard. Doesn't
say much for my ability to connect with
folks, right?

I used to think Raffaella and D were
totally different in every way, but with more
time in the street, I saw there were some
similarities, at least in how they felt about
saving people. In a city of bloodsuckers,
Raffaella and D both kept an eye out for
those weak from being bitten. The huge difference was that Rafi still nibbled after she
saved you, and she was a casual victim herself. D, my dog, always had a bottle of holy
water to pour on your wounds and, behind
closed doors, to heal his own.

D once saved my life, so I obviously
believe the man is pure of heart. Maybe
that's not the best way to judge character. A

bad person can save your life as easily as a
good one. About four years ago at a club
called Cheetah on Twenty-first Street, a female promoter gave cool Monday night hip-hop
parties. Her rule was that early in the evening (roughly 11 P.M. to 1 A.M.) she wouldn't
let in more than two men at a time. Since I
was well behaved and cute, I never had a
problem. Knowing how knuckleheaded the hip-
hop hard core could be, I usually left by
one-thirty and never stayed later than two.

One night I met D, who wasn't yet a mini-
mogul of security. He was hanging out with
Bovine Winslow, the Knicks's power forward
(who later dated Beth Ann). At that point D
was still working the door at a few clubs and
did security for a few minor celebrities like
Winslow. We were standing next to the bar
when we both scoped these big-butt, dark
chocolate sisters in matching blue snakeskin
pants and elaborately braided hair.

We clocked the sisters and talked basketball and the party scene. D told me he was
helping an English promoter named Emily get
the word out about the Tea Party, which eventually blew up to become one of the Apple's
hottest parties. I told him of my R&B dreams
and intimated, but didn't outright tell him,
about my night work. D obviously wasn't as
tall as Bovine, yet he was the one with the

presence, radiating an intense kindness just
below the surface of his large frame. It was
as if D's body was an elaborate camouflage to
conceal the powerfully nice guy underneath.
My man had a strange inner light, a kind of
damaged niceness, as if his kindness was the
result of pain and that these battling ele-
ments were twisted up inside him like elec-
trical wires.

As the night unfolded it became clear I'd
made the better choice when it came to the
snakeskin sistas. The one I favored, Keisha,
was talkative and friendly; D's target, Kamera, had a nasty edge and a sharp tone. D
quickly gave up on Kamera while I ended up
chillin' with Keisha most of the night. What
I didn't know was that Kamera's 'tude, combined with the skintight pants, had attracted
a lot of attention. As harder heads rolled
in, many tried to kick game to Kamera and she
was cold-blooded in cutting them down.

Two-thirty rolled around and the crowd
was growing aggressive, like any male-domi-
nated hip-hop crowd will. D and Bovine hit
the bricks and I scooped up Keisha and Kamera, offering to walk them to their car,
which was parked in a lot down the block. On
the way out of Cheetah, a hulking brother in
a skully and a diamond-studded cross grabbed
Kamera's arm and she said, in her softest

tone, "Nigga, are you crazy!" and jerked herself away.

I was already at the door with Keisha so
at first the dis didn't register. Kamera
caught up to us, muttering about "nasty niggas," but I ignored her and concentrated on
Keisha. But you can never underestimate the
fragility of the urban male's ego. In an era
of instant gratification and music-video role
modeling, where a nice girl could become a
"Be-yatch!" in a heartbeat, dissing a young
man in public could have extreme conse-
quences. The dude in the skully and an
equally large pal exited Cheetah behind us,
shouting endearments like "Who you think you
are, you stuck up stunt!?" By the time we
reached the lot, they were on our heels.

Now I was in a bad position. These guys
were acting in a threatening manner toward
two women I had just met. Gallantry suggested
I stand up for them. Ghetto wisdom said otherwise. I mean, I owed them no allegiance,
and one of the girls I didn't even like. With
tepid enthusiasm I stepped forward and said,
"C'mon man, lighten up. It's not worth all
this stress."

"Stress!" the skully dude shouted and
then peered at me like I was a steaming pile
of shit. "These bitches ain't stressing me,

motherfucker. You're stressing me." The other
guy shifted right, to the edge of my eye
line. I moved sideways to keep both in my
field of vision. Kamera, who had instigated
this situation, looked excited, and Keisha
looked vaguely impressed. Me? I was scared. I
could feel the sweat rolling down my forehead
and building up under my arms.

The second guy accidentally bumped into
Kamera, who not only refused to move out of
his way but then swung at him, which made
Keisha move toward him aggressively, which
made me move toward them, which led the dude
in the skully to coldcock me to the back of
the head and send me tumbling down.

Rule No. 1 of ghetto scrapping is to stay
on your feet. Young brothers can't box like
they used to, but in the age of Tims and Lugz
they'll stomp your ass with great gusto.
Every time I tried to get up, a boot pushed
me down and another banged my ribs or back.
Blood filled my mouth. My right eye closed. I
was verging on unconsciousness and worse. A
foot was headed toward my face and then suddenly it wasn't. I looked over my shoulder
and saw a man throw my skully-wearing
attacker to the ground with a WWF-quality
body slam and then bum rush the other into
the broad side of an SUV. The alarm started

beeping, and after a right, a left, and
another right to the body, the second fool
slumped heavily to the ground.

"Come on, my man," D said as he lifted me
up. "Time to go." He put one of my arms
around his shoulders and guided my wobbly
legs down the street. A couple of hours later
I was released from St. Vincent's with a
black eye, a bruised back, and a broken finger. Waiting outside in the chilly dawn, D
stood looking undertaker grim. I thanked him
profusely and he accepted my words with grace
before helping me haul my damaged pieces back
home.

"I owe you big time, man," I told him.

"You owe me nothing," D said. "If you'd
been stomping on those two motherfuckers I'd
have helped them. I hate seeing people get
taken advantage of. I'm just glad it was you
and not me who picked up Keisha."

"Who?" I said dismissively. "I'm doing my
best to forget their names."

"Okay, my man, but some people might
think she owes you some pussy." Then D smiled
and added, "I'm glad you're not one of those
people."

Over the next four years I saw D rise up
and create D Security, a company that not
only provided club security and bodyguards
for celebrities but, from what I'd been hear-

ing, he had begun dabbling in some low-level detective work. Maybe D was just a scumbag with a heart of gold, but I didn't think so. He never said much about his childhood. I knew he was from Brooklyn and that he was the only child of a broken home. Other than that, he wouldn't volunteer and I got a feeling he'd prefer you didn't ask.

Now, Raffaella loved to tell her life story, or at least a particular version. How much was the truth? A bit, but I'm damn sure not all. According to this tale, her first boyfriend, when she was a kid living outside Rome, was white. He was the boy who popped her cherry. He was the guy she pined for at night. He was the guy whose picture she drew hearts around. Mario was fifteen, she was twelve and well on her way to becoming his bambino for life.

When Rafi was thirteen, she and her father went into Rome to buy a birthday present for her mother. They passed a group of American GIs who were posing in front of a fountain, and that's when Raffaella saw her first black man. The GI was stocky and muscular and wore his army cap low over his eyes. He was very dark and had what Rafi now recognizes as a Southern accent. She remembers making eye contact with him and the GI tipping his cap at her. Rafi stopped dead in her tracks and, despite her father's scolding, didn't move until he pulled her away. Her father resumed his search for a gift, but fair Raffaella was on a new mission. That day by the fountain, she became a BMW aka a black-man woman.

Raffaella began purchasing R&B records from the States, reggae from Jamaica and the U.K., and dance music from West Africa. Not for the music really but the pictures and the attitude. Her parents wrote it off as a phase, but Mario, who knew her soul better than they did, saw it for what it was. One day when Raffaella was mooning over Marvin Gaye's "Sexual Healing," Mario, cursing "moulayans" left and right, ripped Bob Marley and Fela's pictures off her wall. Exit Mario.

Enter Randu, who was spending the summer in Rome with his cosmopolitan big sister, a black model who married an Italian photographer. Randu was sixteen and Raffaella fourteen when they met at an outdoor café that had a jukebox banging the Gap Band, Freddie Jackson, and Shalamar. Randu's Italian was crude; Raffaella's English was rudimentary. Thankfully, both spoke the language of teenage hormones.

Their differences were so exciting. Randu's lips were so large and succulent. His hair was coarse and thick. His ass was

rounder than hers. She loved the smooth way
he danced. She swooned at the cool way he
walked. In essence, Raffaella fell in love
with Randu's surfaces. For her, his body and
all his movements suggested a wide world of
experience and emotion that couldn't be found
in the ancient splendor of Rome.

Next stop for Raffaella would be the
American pillar of civilization—Philadelphia. She got to America the same way generations of attractive European girls have—she
ran off with an African-American soldier.
Lawrence "Be Lo" Boston was a sergeant first
class from Philly who'd learned enough Italian to say "I love you. I need you. I want
you" with appropriate passion. Sure, Be Lo
had a little daughter back home, but he
wasn't married, and hey, Raffaella was his
"dream girl."

Cut to: a naive, twenty-year-old blond
Italian girl living in a Philadelphia housing
project with Be Lo's doting born-again mother
and his three kids, with regular visits by
all three babies' mothers, each of whom was
seeking her rightful piece of Be Lo's U.S.
Army check. Be Lo, now based at a camp in
central Pennsylvania, was away for weeks at a
time and, mysteriously, rarely let Rafi
visit, suggesting there may have been another
woman in the mix. Of course, it got ugly

fast. At various times each of the mothers
took a swing at Raffaella—two connected. Her
command of American curse words grew exponen-
tially.

Salvation, of a sort, came in the form of
Marjorie Watkins, a budding hip-hop chicken-
head working at Jersey Turnpike strip clubs
in order to feed her daughter. Raffaella
wasn't sure about being nude in public, but
after Randu's baby mother No. 2 threatened to
cut off her blond locks (and use it in a
weave!), home girl broke out. Though inexpe-
rienced and nervous, Raffaella's Italian
accent titillated the customers, and tips
were massive. As a strip team called Salt &
Pepa, Raffaella and Marjorie began performing
private gigs where Raffaella's interest in
brown-eyed handsome men was reciprocated.

Here's where Raffaella's tale gets
screwy. She claims she "never ever" worked as
a prostitute. Okay, fine. She also claims a
man at a private party later introduced her
to a fiftyish white woman named Mildred who,
because "we saw life the same," taught Rafi
the ins and outs of upscale brothel management. That a high-level madam would school a
nonhooker seems crazy. "You mean you didn't
sell any ass for this lady?" I used to ask.
Rafi would just roll her eyes and say, "You
just do not understand," and she was right.

However she did it, Raffaella transformed herself from a military bride into a very successful proprietor of a high-end escort service. When Raffaella recruited me, she'd been in business seven years. She still had a noticeable Italian accent and the same wide-eyed demeanor that got her to America in the first place, but by now what was once natural was mostly game.

Raffaella had been my savior. She took my reckless sexual energy and gave it focus, and I owed her for that. But she didn't love me (nor I her), and Raffaella certainly was not my mother (though sometimes she acted like it). In the end, we both got something out of it, which made it a great business deal, but hopefully, not the foundation of my life.

The Voice That Woke Me Up

The voice that woke me up belonged to a woman: "I have work for you, Night." Her tone was, as always, a command and a seduction. You could take it either way and still be right.

"When and where?" I mumbled.

"Silver Cup Studios," Bee Cole told me. "Be there by noon."

"My usual rate?" I inquired.

"Maybe even a bonus," she said. The clock read 7 A.M. When I opened my eyes again it was 11:15 A.M., and I dragged myself into the shower. I made good time out to Long Island City, an area of Queens just over the Fifty-ninth Street Bridge and home to a medley of arts institutions like the contemporary art museum P.S. 1, the Center for Motion Pictures, and Silver Cup, where movies, commercials, and music videos were all shot.

Bee Cole was doing a two-day extravaganza based around Andnet, an Aaliyah wannabe signed to Powerful Music. I was to be one of three men vying for her love.

In my section I was her boho lover and was given a tam, leather sandals, and a blue T-shirt with a *Mod Squad* logo on it.

When I arrived on set, Bee was in full director mode. No glamour outfit. No cooing convo. Just Bee ruling over her loyal crew of gaffers, grips, and gofers. When I came over for wardrobe approval she said, "You need to start getting some sleep, Night. Beauty fades, you know." She turned to the stylist, a small slender gal with fluffy orange hair and matching shades, and said, "I hate that T-shirt. Get him something mustard colored and made of hemp. And make sure it shows his chest." Then Bee gave me a kiss on the cheek and walked over to chew a hole in the production designer's ass.

After Bee's dismissal I headed straight to the makeup trailer for a serious touch-up. Inside, Maybelle Lewis, an old-school makeup diva with bone-straight hair, small Asian eyes, and big, baby cheeks, was studying Polaroids of Andnet's face. "Oh, no," Maybelle shouted when she saw me, in one of those patented black woman exclamations of overdone joy. "Come here and give me some sugar." After giving me a life-threatening hug, Maybelle guided me into a chair that was set before a brightly lit makeup mirror. I could hear her humming as she surveyed my face. "Baby, you need to treat yourself better," she said. "Or get you a new woman, 'cause I can see worry all over your face."

Maybelle began applying makeup to the areas under my eyes. I noticed a *New York Post* on the floor by my feet with a typically subtle headline, PARK AVE SEX SLAY, and a photo of a white woman in a high-society gown. Maybelle followed my eye line to the paper. "Oh, yeah, that's a wild story."

"Tell me."

"Rich old white lady was found choked on a black dildo by the maid. She was all done up in a black leather corset. As if that wasn't enough, the woman was found wearing a Billie Holiday mask. Rich white folks are something else."

I tried to push her aside gently. "Let me see the paper."

"Hold on," she said as she continued applying makeup.

"No," I insisted and moved Maybelle out of the way. I held the paper close to my face.

"Damn, Night, you sure do love a scandal."

The lurid story contained one frightening detail: Mr. Perl was in Columbus, Ohio, on business at the time of the murder. Ohio? There were no witnesses to the crime, though the police said they had suspects. My mind whirled back to the masks, the pushy ass husband (who apparently wasn't), the silent black dominatrix, the double-header sex, my throwing down the money, and Raffaella's anxiety.

"Night," Maybelle said, breaking my concentration, "if you keep looking like that I'm gonna have to use a lot of pancake." Ignoring her, I two-wayed Raffaella, but the server replied that her E address was no longer in the system. As Maybelle stood by irritated, I dialed Rafi's cell phone and then her land line. Both were disconnected.

After that, I wasn't really focused on acting sexy with a barely postpubescent wanna-be pop star. I was rather listless on the set, which upset Andnet, since it seemed an unflattering commentary on her sex appeal. In between sets up Bee pulled me aside.

"I don't know what's up with you, but get over it, Night."

"Something bad's going on, Bee."

"Are you dying of something?"

"No."

"Then get over it. This video is for the people interested in signing you. They wanna see how you flow with that child they've invested millions in. Right now the vibe would be negative. Very negative."

"I realize that."

"Good," Bee said and then added, "The next multimillion-dollar video I shoot should be for you, Night. Help me make that happen."

So for the next couple of hours I pulled it together, smiling wider, flirting better, and acting like the black American gigolo I was, not just another scared nigga. By the time I was wrapped, Andnet (real name: Andrea Johnson) was slipping me her cell number and Bee Cole was squeezing my butt like a ripe melon. For a moment everything was as it should have been.

Still, worry was grinding a hole in my stomach. I had to track down Raffaella and find out the real deal on Park Avenue. A young black hustler connected to a rich dead white woman? That's a problem.

I took a cab from Queens up to Raffaella's West Side apartment. As I walked toward her building's front door I was still wiping bits of stale makeup off my face. That's probably why I, a man who prides himself on being streetwise, was caught unaware as two plainclothes cops pinned my arms behind me.

"What's going on?" I shouted. "What did I do?"

The younger of the two cops, a ruddy-faced white man in a brown suit with one of those pointy, dirty-blond surfer dude haircuts, ignored me and yelled over my shoulder, "Is this him?"

Raffaella stuck her blond head out of the window of an ugly blue unmarked car and nodded. "Yes," she said weakly. "That is Night."

"Let Me Get This Straight"

"Let me get this straight, young Mr. Night with an N, not a K," said the dapper black detective. "You fuck rich white women for a living?"

"Well," I said and then stammered. "Ah, well, kinda. Some would say that, I guess."

"Well, I need to meet your employment agency," he said with a laugh and toyed with his tie. He wore expensive, well-shined Italian loafers and an extremely well-tailored gray suit. "But wait, Night with an N," he said, "I have already met your employment agency, haven't I? Not a bad looking career counselor, Night. Not bad at all."

I didn't wanna acknowledge that Detective Tyrone Williams was right. He knew he was. He was just testing me. He wanted to see my eyes jump and my body shift and my lips wobble. He was an old cop with a receding hairline, gray hair, and these steely tinted glasses. Very well dressed, as I said, and imposing. He looked like a man who was used to wearing good clothes, and it apparently gave him pleasure.

"What are you staring at, Mr. Night?"

"Ah, your suit, Detective. You dress very well."

He ran one hand across his jacket and said, "Very observant of you."

I wasn't sure if or when an attorney would show up. Normally I would have called Raffaella, but that clearly wasn't an option and wouldn't be ever again. I thought of calling one of my clients but knew better. My sister was at the hospital with my father and I couldn't do that. I kinda didn't believe it, but I ended up calling Beth Ann. Got her answering machine. Left a message concerning my sad scenario, my whereabouts, and my legal needs: I also suggested she contact Adebonojo for me, though in retrospect that's who I should have called in the first place.

Hindsight is perfect so I just had to live with my decision and wait things out. Detective Williams paced around me as he talked. The white cop who'd cuffed me on the street sat in a chair across from me, looking on like a student.

"So, Mr. Night," the old black man began, "you were at the Park Avenue home of Nathaniel and Audrey Perl on the morning of Tuesday, October 10, 2002. Isn't that right?"

"Yes, sir," I responded politely. We then went through the details of that night, which he already knew most of. But Detective Williams didn't know some of the same things I didn't.

"So," he asked again, "you never saw the face of the black woman behind the Billie Holiday mask?"

"No. She never took the mask off and she only spoke once. But everybody seemed very comfortable with each other. I got the vibe that she'd been there before. Did you ask Raffaella about her?"

"Of course, Mr. Night," he answered. But that was all the detective was gonna tell me. He continued, "And you didn't come back the next morning, this morning, and visit the Perls?"

"No, sir."

"So where were you between 11:30 P.M. and 1:30 A.M.?"

"I was at Man Ray having dinner and then I went to the hospital to see my father and then I went to Beth Ann's apartment."

"The gigolo and the supermodel, huh?" the detective said with a sly smile. "This is some life you're having, young man. Some life, indeed. The problem is, we haven't been able to contact the young lady. The next problem is that we have found a cab driver who picked you up at Bellevue and dropped you off on 116th Street. What were doing up there, Mr. Night? Buying crack?" The two cops found that funny.

While they chuckled, my mind raced. I had a solid alibi—two witnesses who could say I was nowhere near the scene of the crime. The three of us were together in Harlem for much of those two hours. The rest of it was spent with Beth Ann in the taxi heading downtown. Except, of course, that we were having a discussion about drug trafficking and kidnapping.

"The driver must be mistaken," I offered weakly.

"Maybe he'd be mistaken about you," Detective Williams replied. "Just another young black man with unruly hair. But cab drivers don't usually forget driving a woman from the *Sports Illustrated* swimsuit issue."

"I think I should speak to a lawyer."

The detective seemed amused and said, "That's well within your rights. A Legal Aid lawyer will be around in the morning. Tonight you'll be a guest of the City of New York and a potential suspect in a Murder One case."

"Murder One." My shoulders sagged. I sighed. Blood rushed to my head.

"Think about it, Mr. Night. Male hustler comes back

to the scene of a previous job, one that ended badly, for money and revenge. He takes his hostility out on the wife. Maybe you lost your head in the heat of the moment—maybe you came in to do harm."

"I didn't do that, Detective."

"Well, Mr. Night without the K, you did something you don't wanna tell me about. Maybe you'll be more forthcoming in the morning. Good night." He smiled. "You must get that a lot, huh?"

I was more scared this time in jail than I was when I was a kid. Back then I knew I was being framed but felt the truth would come out. Now I was old enough to understand that the truth might not set me free. The thought that the next time Nikki saw me would be behind glass in a baggy uniform with unlaced shoes made me wanna cry. The minute I stepped into that holding pen I knew fear was flying off me. There were half a dozen men in the area—all of them black and Latino, all of them harder looking than me, all of them likely veterans of this no-win game. Still, no one said shit to me. Didn't seem like there was any posse in this particular cell. Lots of lonely, depressed individuals keeping their own counsel.

Except for one guy. He was Latino and had on a

black Allen Iverson jersey and black sweatpants with
white piping and black Iverson Reeboks. He had a black
doo rag on his head and a soul patch under his mouth.
He was a handsome guy with big lips and thick eye-
brows. When he smiled at me a chill ran down my spine
that would freeze ice cubes.

As he came toward me a few guys looked over, perhaps hoping for a bit of action to cut through the bore-
dom. I knew a smile could be as lethal as a frown in a
street situation, and jail was the ultimate street. I'd seen
gunshots follow many a false grin.

The closer the Latino got, the more familiar he
became. Older, a bit battered, yet still handsome and a
bit fey, the man approaching me was J-Luv. "What's up,
Night?" he said in a hoarse, tired voice. "Yo man, it's
me. J-Luv."

We stood there a moment, measuring each other.
Then I said, "It's been a long time, man. We should
catch up. I guess we have time, right?"

"No doubt," he said.

I squatted and rested my back against the bars. He
did the same. J-Luv did most of the talking and didn't fall
silent until daylight peeped through a window.

"GOD DON'T LIKE UGLY"

Before she died, my mother used to say, "God don't like ugly," in response to anything that displeased her. And I heard it often around the house, because my father was always doing or saying something she didn't like. As I listened to J-Luv, my mother's words echoed in my head.

Yes, J-Luv admitted he did brick me. The revelation of his convo was that it started way before that fateful weekend. He'd been laying the groundwork for my downfall for months.

"I was getting jealous of you, Night," he admitted in the cell that night. "You were green and probably didn't realize what was going down, but you were moving up in the eyes of promoters. They were inviting you to gigs they didn't invite me to. You were singing to the bitches and I couldn't compete with that. Plus, you had two women fighting over you and willing to support your young ass. I had my gifts and shit, but hell, nigga, I was still living with my mother."

He'd been quietly fueling the anxiety both Anasette and Florence had been feeling since the fight. He'd whisper in the ear of one and visit the other with some incriminating tale. So when I didn't come back to New York after that Jersey gig, J-Luv saw his big chance to pour more salt on my game. He made Anasette crazy by telling her I was leaving her for that white girl in Jersey. She should have fluffed it off but my absence, and my arrogance at not calling, pushed her over the edge and she broke out with another stripper for Miami.

To Florence he told one incredible lie—that Anasette and I were moving to Jersey to live in a condo apartment paid for by that same chick. She should have laughed in J-Luv's face but she took the hook. This silly tale fed into Florence's own insecurity about Anasette, about possessing me, and some deep-seated envy/hatred of white women I knew nothing about but that J-Luv, like Iago in *Othello*, had peeped and exploited.

I guess my reaction should have been anger. The man had dogged me well. Yet this part of J-Luv's tale just made me laugh. It was another life. I couldn't be mad now. Plus, I'd always known that I was in over my head handling those two women. J-Luv had just confirmed that truth.

However, J-Luv's victory proved fleeting. Not a month after I disappeared into Raffaella's world, J-Luv snorted heroin for the first time. He tried to blame it on guilt—he was haunted by what he'd done to me, etc., etc.—but we both knew that was bullshit. Once we got past that, J-Luv admitted he got strung out lovely on horse's beatific ride and started saddling up regularly.

While I was occupied learning the gigolo trade, J-Luv got deeper into gay trick & treat. The money was steady and solid, and being high made the job demands palatable. Pretty soon J-Luv was running full-color ads in the back of *The Village Voice* and the *New York Press* of his flat stomach and boxers with copy that announced, LATIN LOVER LOOSE.

"I didn't have time to be romancing some old dried-up bitch," he said in justification. "I needed to hit it and quit it, you know."

Like many a whore before him, the drugs fed J-Luv's need for dollars and the dollars enabled him to cop. A couple of blurry, semen-soaked years went by. Then J-Luv heard about my new gig and the lifestyle. So he stepped to Ramon about getting hooked up with the infamous Raffaella. Ramon laughed at him. J-Luv's addiction disqualified him from upper-class employment. Plus, he was told they already had a Latino who did gay tricks. "We got that demo covered," Ramon told him and then laughed in his face.

It was back to heroin and gay strip clubs and a lifestyle that landed him in jail. I didn't ask precisely why he was in jail. It was clear he'd been caught sucking the wrong dick or having his sucked or something like that. I sure didn't need the details. J-Luv whined but did not cry as he related all this. No, he left the crying to me.

Not because I was sorry for him but, I guess, because I was sorry for me. If I hadn't hooked up with this fool, I just would have been trying to sing. I would have been just another cute guy trying to be a sex symbol. That would have occupied all my time. That would have been my only activity and my deepest ambition.

Instead I'd followed this freak's lead and taken a long, strange trip. And the thing that was truly sad and funny, the thing that made me cry, was, here we were in the same motherfucking jail cell. All my Richard-Gere-black, rich-white-woman, rich-young-privileged-girl adventures didn't amount to shit. I'd sold my body for sex. So had J-Luv. And we were both in a New York City jail cell and I was in way more trouble than he was. That was something to cry about.

I'VE ALWAYS LOVED BEING IN THE SPOTLIGHT

I've always loved being in the spotlight. As a kid I was a real showoff, doing my moonwalk and singing "Billie Jean" at the appearance of any doting adult. It's what made me uninhibited enough to strip, insecure enough to seek stardom, and vain enough to work as a gigolo.

But on the morning after being detained in connection with the Perl murder, I was in a nasty ass spotlight on a long narrow stage with bright lights, a dingy supporting cast, and an audience you desperately wanted to ignore you. This particular venue was called Police Lineup. I did not want to be the star of this show.

It was strangely reassuring that J-Luv was in the lineup with me. He'd done so much evil in his life, I hoped his aura would catch the eye of the witnesses behind the glass. Probably the doorman from the other night. Some taxi drivers. Maybe Mr. Perl himself, who was conveniently out of town the night it went down. That's the freak who should have been up here with me. But Mr.

Perl lived on Park Avenue and I resided in Alphabet City. Because of my fleeting encounter with Audrey Perl, whom I was never formally introduced to, I was staring at a one-way mirror and the eyes of hidden accusers. That half hour in a Miles Davis mask could have been the most important thirty minutes of my life.

My lineup comrades were two nondescript white men at either end, a potbellied bald-headed brother on my left and J-Luv to my right. I was the only person in that space who fit the description of a tall, dark black man with a brushy natural haircut. I was surely being set up. No question about that. I just sighed, looked into the lights, and tried to look innocent.

When it was my turn to step forward, I looked straight ahead and then stepped back. It was surprisingly perfunctory. Next up was J-Luv. Not only did my old buddy step forward, he was asked to turn to his left and then to his right. I could feel his eyes on my face as he turned in profile. And I saw fear. I didn't blame him. This was not what we'd expected. And then it hit me. A bolt of genuine revelation that could save my ass and maybe J-Luv's as well.

As we walked out, J-Luv whispered to me, "What the fuck was that?"

"You're Latino," I answered, "that's what's up."

"What do you mean?"

"I'll tell you back in the pen."

That conversation never happened. As we entered the hallway, the young white surfer-dude detective took me by the arm and guided me away from J-Luv. I wanted to say something slick like "Did I pass the audition?" but I was too scared to front. We entered the same interview room as the day before. Detective Williams was smoking a cigar. Standing next to him was my man D. I damn near leaped into his arms. Instead I just gave him a hug and said, "Oh, man, it's good to see you."

"Yeah, but not in here."

"This is lovely," the detective interrupted. "Black men bonding. It makes me proud."

D ignored the detective and said to me, "Every man's dick gets him in trouble but you've taken it to a whole 'nother level, Night."

"Yeah," I agreed.

Detective Williams told us to sit down. D sat between myself and the cop, and his presence took the pomp out of Williams. He wasn't as arch or at ease. Still, he peppered me with a new set of questions: "Did Raffaella need money?" "What are the names of Raffaella's other employees?" "Do you have numbers on any of them?" Without saying it explicitly, Detective Williams revealed I was no longer a murder suspect.

Feeling less defensive and quite relieved, I volunteered some info: "The guy who stood next to me in the lineup, J-Luv, has been in this game a long time. Well, he reminded me of this guy who worked for Raffaella. His name is Enrique. Don't know his last name. But he was buck wild. He'd do anything for cash. I could see Raffaella using him when I wouldn't go back. He's got a bad temper and is kinda mean. If your witnesses were interested in J-Luv they could have really been thinking of Enrique."

Detective Williams listened and nodded. "Well, thank you, Mr. Night. I appreciate the information." He cut the surfer detective a look but to me he was still a menacing blank. Continuing, he said, "Now I must admit, Night, I'm still very curious about what you, Miss Beth Ann, and a Mr. Simon Adebonojo were meeting about on 116th Street. A supermodel, a male hustler, and an African scam artist must have lots of common interests."

I hadn't mentioned Adebonojo. The cop had figured out who we'd gone to see, which means I'd put my friend in jeopardy. Despite being a naturalized citizen the Nigerian-born businessman still felt vulnerable to both the police and the INS, even if he was doing nothing, and obviously Adebonojo was not a man who was doing nothing.

"However," the detective added, "I do not have the time and the manpower right now to investigate that gathering. Our mutual friend assures me of your high character and that of the model."

D snapped, "Are you through with him, Fly Ty?"

"No, I am not!" he snapped back. I jumped in my seat. The two men stared at each other through what seemed to be years of hostility. "Not until you call me by my title. Then your friend here can leave."

D sucked back his anger and looked down at his lap. After a very tense moment, D said, "Can I take Night with me, Detective Tyrone Williams?"

"Anytime you wish," was the answer.

I didn't look at the detective or say good-bye. I hopped out of my seat and headed straight for the door. I kept my mouth shut as I was processed out of custody and walked back out into New York City, a shaky but liberated soul.

At a nearby Kentucky Fried Chicken I spilled my guts to D about Beth Ann, Raffaella, my father, my singing—

all the contradictory and tangled events of the previous three days. He grunted, nodded, and at times looked quite upset. D's ability to be empathic was surely tested by what I told him.

When I'd finally stopped babbling, D told me, "From now on, you let me know when trouble comes, okay? Don't hold back. If you let me, I'll help you. I know a lot of people. Just let me know, okay?

"Now," he said next, "you need to go home, take a shower, and get some sleep. Then you need to go see your father. Forget the bullshit—that's the most important thing happening in your life right now. My father and I are separated—have been since I was little. I understand your pain but you don't have to have it. Go see him. Go be with your family." Then his tone changed from consoling to slightly desperate. "Now, where is Beth Ann?"

I pulled out my two-way. There were messages from Raffaella, my sister, and three from Beth Ann. All of them were from numbers I didn't recognize. "According to the times here, she hasn't called since yesterday afternoon or after I was arrested."

I wrote the numbers on his notepad. He sipped his coffee and looked down at the numbers. Suddenly he looked indecisive. He wanted to dial up Beth Ann, but then D, who a moment earlier had been so strong, now seemed as shaky as I'd been at the station.

"Listen," he said, "I'll call her later. You get some sleep, okay?"

"D, how did you know where I was?"

D laughed and told me, "Man, you are a star. The *Post* has a picture with you and some old rich-looking white lady, and it's not on Page Six, Holmes. They ran a piece about a male hustler suspected in a murder case."

"Oh, shit. I'm through. That'll kill everything I'm doing. No more clients. No more record deal."

"Hey, man, you could have been accused of Murder One," he replied. "You just dodged the real bullet, so you better enjoy that. I've known Fly Ty since I was kid. Night, you gotta know, if he wanted you, you'd be toast. You just lucked out that he called me for some info on the club scene and I happened to be tight with you. Otherwise this could have all gone down very different."

"You two don't seem to like each other."

"That's a long story, Night. We don't have enough daylight left to tell it and I wouldn't talk about it after dark. You feel me?"

"I guess," I said, but I really didn't understand what

he meant. "Hey," I asked, "was your word enough to clear me of suspicion?"

"That and the fact you were innocent. You *are* innocent, right?"

"No, D, I'm not innocent. Just not guilty. We both know I haven't been innocent in years."

On the way home I purchased a *Post* and was, I gotta admit, kinda proud. The *Post* photo was actually flattering. I was in an Armani suit escorting Polly at a gallery opening in Chelsea. I was smiling. She was smiling. Don't know why we were so happy, but we sure looked it. The headline read, BLACK AMERICAN GIGOLO, and the caption talked about my "alleged" male hustler activities and my questioning in connection with the Perl murder. I felt for Polly. Her phone must be burning up and her kids in an uproar. All my other clients had to be ducking for cover or simply erasing my number from their Palm Pilots. And what must Nikki and my father think?

Though I was dead tired and sprawled out on my bed, I still tried to reach Nikki but got no answer on her cell or pager. Just left messages. So I cut them both off and closed my eyes. It was late afternoon when I opened them again. I'd slept most of the day. Still I was tired. My sleep had not refreshed me. It didn't help one bit that I woke up to Raffaella sitting on a chair, staring at me and sipping wine. It was eerily reminiscent of the first time we met. The difference was, instead of me needing her, she needed me.

"What the fuck are you doing here?"

"I needed a place to stay," she said, very matter-of-factly, like there was no other place she should be. "You gave me a key for emergencies, Night. Remember?"

"You can't stay here," I said, sitting up. "Not after you turned me in."

"No!" She came over to the bed and tried to squeeze next to me. "They knew about you. They knew you'd been to see the Perls and they made me ID you. I had no choice. They think you might have gone back. I told them you hadn't, but they had their own ideas. I would never have gotten you in trouble, Night."

I looked her in the eyes and said, "Enrique told them, huh?"

Raffaella recoiled and breathed heavily, "No! There's no way he would have done that. He's scared himself."

"A murderer should be scared."

"Enrique," she said defiantly, "did not kill that woman."

Sounding like a cop, I damn near shouted, "And how do you know?"

"He says he thinks Billie Holiday did it," she answered. "He says she was there when he left, along with Mr. Perl."

"Mr. Perl? Mr. Perl was in Cincinnati on business. He wasn't there. That's what the papers said. As for Billie Holiday, she struck me as a real pro, while Enrique is a fool and a liar." I got out of bed and walked over to the refrigerator. "Between you two, why should I believe a word?"

Raffaella sprang from the bed and was on me before I could open the refrigerator door. "Listen, Night," she said with desperation, "I'm scared." She grabbed ahold of me for dear life. "They let me go as some kind of decoy. They think the killer will kill me or something. I can't be alone. I don't know why they treat me this way. Is it because I'm Italian?"

I almost laughed at that. "It's because you're the pimp who knows too much. And as for staying here, hell no! The police are probably outside right now thinking who knows what." Raffaella just started crying big, huge boo-hoo tears.

Just then, as if on cue, someone rang my front-door buzzer.

"Who is it?" I asked through the intercom.

"Let me in." Fuck. I buzzed Beth Ann in. She entered like a wounded animal, unsteady and tired. There were bags under her lovely eyes. She was nervous. Her first words were, "I'm sorry," and then she embraced me. I didn't embrace back. She saw Raffaella and Raffaella saw her. Raffaella's first words were, "I love your work."

Beth Ann's second words were, "Who's this?"

Raffaella's second words were, "I'm his pimp. My name is Raffaella."

So I sat there in my underwear with these women, the homeless pimp and the not-so-supermodel, both of whom had reshaped my life. Beth Ann sat down and didn't mention D, so I decided not to either. Let her play it her way. When she took her jacket off there was a big, nasty bruise on her right arm.

Raffaella, genuinely appalled, asked, "Who would do that to you?"

I answered for her: "The big nasty men she's doing business with, right?"

"Yes," she said sadly. "I saw Maura."

"And?" I said.

"They have her on some kind of drug. Maybe heroin, I don't know." Her face, already sad, sagged further. "Night, I think they've taken advantage of her. They took the money from me and they expect more. A lot more. Have you spoken to Adebonojo? How's it going?"

"No," I replied, icy as hell. "I've been in police custody. I left you messages."

"I know." Her face shifted again. She became appropriately remorseful and contrite. "I was scared, Night. I was afraid to help."

From behind me Raffaella volunteered, "I'm sure that's true, Night. She seems like such a nice girl."

That was it. I'd had enough. "Fuck this," I told them. "I'm taking a shower. Talk amongst yourselves."

Under the water I strategized. I needed to do some reconnaissance, marshal my forces, and take as much control as possible of the situation. I peeked out of the shower and saw that the ladies had bonded a bit, sharing wine as Raffaella applied ice to Beth Ann's arm. I walked past them, back to my studio, where I made several phone calls.

Then I got dressed and told my guests, "Ladies, it's time to go. I have a place for you to stay tonight."

Almost in unison they asked, "Where will you be tonight?"

I mumbled, "Somewhere," and ushered them out of my apartment.

*   *   *

Ted was ecstatic. I've never seen a man so happy to have an alleged criminal and murder suspect in his home. When we arrived, his son, Tad, wanted to play. Rosie had cooked dinner. Ted brought me back to his studio for a private chat. He asked, "Is what the papers say true?"

"Yeah," I said. "They suspected me of murder but that's dead now."

"And," he said looking me dead in the eye, "the rest?"

"Not really," I said lying easily. "I got a gift or two from women, Ted. But a black *American Gigolo*? I wish. My dream is to be an R&B singer. It always has been and continues to be, God willing."

"And those two beautiful women in there are just unfortunates caught up in your troubles?"

"Something like that."

He snorted and shook his head. "Wow," Ted began, "you are really full of shit, Night. But I like you. I really do and I know you wouldn't kill a soul." Then he gazed at me quite soulfully and added, "I'll definitely help you, Night. But when this is over we have to have a very frank talk." I agreed and thanked him for his friendship.

Ted leaned in and hugged me, and I made it as chaste as I could.

In the living room Tad looked perfectly happy to have an Italian blonde to play a boxing video game against, and Raffaella looked relieved not to be worrying. Rosie watched me with a hard, appraising eye even as she set the table. Beth Ann still seemed very much on edge. She sat perched in a comfy-looking chair, leafing through but not seeing the pages of *Billboard*.

"I'm scared and I'm tired," she whispered when I came over. "It's like I'm split in half. I'm not letting Ivy or anyone in that world know what's going on, but I'm sure people are aware that I'm falling apart. I bet they're blaming it on drugs."

"And," I said, "they'd be right."

I truly wanted to be sympathetic but there was so much subtext to Beth Ann. Things were happening just outside my understanding, yet I was implicated in them. The Perl murder case seemed cut and dry compared to messing with Beth Ann. "Has D called you?" I wondered.

"Yes," she replied and looked away.

"What's up with you two? Are you lovers, enemies, or what? I can't figure it out."

"It's not complicated," she said, not even trying to lie well. "He was good friends with a guy I used to date—the basketball player. We got to know each other. He thinks he knows me." Then she stopped. That was it. Her explanation of an uncomplicated relationship.

Tad came over and wanted to know if we wanted to join Raffaella and him. I declined but Beth Ann agreed and walked over to the sofa with him. It struck me that Beth Ann and D had at some point fucked but they were never really lovers. Don't know why it hit me like that. That distinction seemed like splitting hairs. But it felt right to me. One of them wanted more (probably D) and one was fine with whatever had happened (surely Beth Ann).

If I slept with Beth Ann now, that's what I'd be—a fuck. I'd been that for so many women but I couldn't stand to just be that for her. How you got to be more—her man, her lover—I had no idea. As with Tandi, Beth Ann was a black girl who was out of my league, and no amount of good deeds on my part could change that. Everything I was and did got in the way, and there was no changing that. Maybe when I became an R&B god, I could step to her, though it felt too late. Maybe my past could still be overcome, but no, not with her.

I broke out of Ted's place happy as hell to be alone

again. It was early evening and there was much to do.
First and foremost I had to deal with my family. All the
way out to my father's house I wondered what I'd say.
Would he be embarrassed? Would I, as usual, blame
him before me blamed me? I didn't know.

My sister answered the door and squeezed me like a
teddy bear. I'd been hugged all day—by D, Raffaella,
Beth Ann, Ted—but this was the one I needed. I just sunk
into my little sister. I thought of my mother and how much
I missed her and how much this little woman meant to
me. She took my woolly head in her hands. "I am so
glad you came."

"I hope he is," he said. "I hope I am."

His house, my house, our house still smelled of our old
life: the dust of my comic books; the scent of my first
cologne, Aramis; the hair grease my mother put in her
hair and Nikki's; my father's funk after a day pushing a
mail cart; the cinnamon incense he employed to cover
that funk. I could smell me at seven, at eleven, and at
nineteen. There was a new smell medicinal and sterile,
like the cotton inside a bottle of pills.

My father's room was disconcertingly bright. His TV
was tuned to ESPN. His laptop sat on the bed with an
unfinished chess match on screen. All three of the room's

lamps were on. I'd expected him to be slumped over looking sickly, as at Bellevue. Instead Pops sat up with his spectacles balanced on his nose, a copy of the *Amsterdam News* in his lap, and his gray hair a blinding white. The man didn't look sick—he looked overstimulated.

He said, "Well, well, well," and sized me up. His voice was deep with rust along the edges. It was a baritone that used to move crowds. Now it just rippled across the bedsheets. "Lover man," he said. "Lover man."

I walked over to the bed and stood over him. His chest still puffed out, but his stomach was now round. Those huge dark-brown hands that held bullhorns, shuffled mail, and hugged my mother close reached out to grab his only son. He engulfed me. There was no end to me and no beginning to him—we were one.

His tears dampened my shirt. Mine fell slowly and disappeared into his bright-white hair. Forgive. Apologize. Understand. Explain. Plead. Yell. Argue. Love. Through that embrace, which was stronger than a hug—more like a merging, really—we went through all those emotions. The silence that I'd felt toward my father ended without words.

Yeah, we finally did speak. But they were just words. "Great to see you." "I'm no longer a suspect." "The doctors say I'm gonna be fine." "Yes, I do get a lot of pussy." "Yeah, I expect to retire real soon." "We should visit your mother's grave together." "Yeah, we should." Words are just suggestions of emotions—not the emotions themselves. It was that embrace that made us whole. The words that followed just gave voice to feelings we'd already exchanged.

After all I'd said, after the bad things I believed he let happen to me, after my cruelty at ignoring him, after all those bitter years of anger and spite and a longing that boiled in my stomach, it now seemed simple to admit I loved him. It was strange how easy it was. All it took was his sudden illness, my unexpected incarceration, and the exposure of my secret life in the *New York Post.* You know—everyday stuff.

"Where are you going?" Nikki inquired as she wiped her eyes and stood by the front door an hour later. "It's late, you know."

"What's my name?"

"Neal Daniel Taylor."

"Yeah, okay?" I rolled my eyes. "But what do I call myself?"

Nikki screwed up her face and said, "Something silly." I threw a fake punch toward her face and then took her soft little face in my hands.

"I have a lot of unfinished business. After all—"

"Is this a bad pun coming?"

"The worst." I cleared my throat. "After all, the Night is still young." And, indeed, it was.

"MUCH NIGERIAN BUSINESS"

"These people don't get much Nigerian business," Adebonojo said proudly. "Japanese. Jewish. Arab. Lots of British. But few customers from my country. It's good to know my countrymen aren't swayed by such perversion."

Adebonojo and I sat in a black sedan parked on Twenty-second Street between Ninth and Tenth Avenues, a so-so mix of residential and commercial buildings. One of the residential buildings housed one of the city's most exclusive S&M brothels. At my behest, Adebonojo had spent much of the afternoon supervising visits by employees to S&M brothels all over Manhattan, the majority of which were below Twenty-third Street. So far they'd found no mistress who matched the description of the woman in the Billie Holiday mask. Turned out most of the sisters working at these spots were big fleshy women whose weight made them perfect for latent nanny worship among the white-collar class.

The woman behind the Billie Holiday mask had hips but was otherwise sleek and cool. More the physique of a personal trainer than a biscuit-and-waffle-making servant. We were about to give up looking when D came through for me again. D Security guarded the door at a few upscale brothels around Manhattan, and he thought there was this one high-level lady who fit the mold.

"Calls herself Missy DeMann," D reported. "Fit, strong, with broad shoulders and solid legs," D said. "She's very vocal about only handling white clients, but she has quite a few prominent black men who visit her. The idea that she's making an exception to see brothers is part of her appeal."

Adebonojo was going to see her, in the guise of a visiting Nigerian official. He was outfitted in a crisp gray suit and nice wing tips and had splashed on some overripe cologne. And despite his high-handed words, I knew he was looking forward to this.

"A man will never possess knowledge," he offered, "if he doesn't take time to be a student."

"Yeah, yeah," I said to that bull as the clock neared his midnight appointment. "You just can't wait to lick this sista's boot, can you?" We both laughed at that. Then I asked, "We've been so crazy these last few days that you haven't said anything about how the E sale is going."

"Very well, Night," he said with his wonderful grin. "I believe we'll have made about a hundred thousand dollars by tomorrow night as we sell off what Beth Ann brought us. I'm nervous I won't be able to get my men back into selling counterfeit watches after this."

"My bad," I replied. "I feel awful corrupting you."

"You know," he suggested, "the young lady is lying about something, or certainly not telling the whole truth."

"I know. I know. But I'm still not sure what that might be. Honestly, if I hadn't gotten you involved, I would have walked away by now."

Adebonojo's smile got even wider and more ingratiating. "Keep telling yourself that, Night."

"What?" I said defensively.

"Beth Ann is proof that beauty is the most negotiable currency in the world."

I had no reply to that. He was right and I was a sucka.

Adebonojo was about to head out of the car when Nate Perl walked out of the brownstone. Damn, that man was bold. Had his wife knocked off and was hanging with the killer two days later. I told Adebonojo who it was and he looked at me like I was crazy. "That is not Nate Perl, Night."

"What the fuck are you talking about? That's the man who paid me. That's the man who met me and that's the man who fucked Mrs. Perl and Billie Holiday."

"What paper do you read, young man?"

"What's that got to do with anything?"

"Well, if you read more than the *Post* and looked into the *Times* or the *Daily News* once in a while, or even watched New York 1, you'd have seen that Nate Perl was a tall dark-haired man with a full beard. A man who looks nothing like the gentleman coming down the block." The Mr. Perl that I knew walked in our direction and then opened the door to a steel-gray Saab.

"Are you sure, Adebonojo?"

"Absolutely, Night."

I bit my lip. I sighed deeply. I needed a new plan. I needed to read more papers. "Listen," I said, "go in and do as we planned. Get a reading on this woman and I'll follow Mr. Perl or whoever he is. Call me when you're through."

My Mr. Perl didn't drive very far. He went down Ninth Avenue into the Meatpacking District, once a place of butcher shops, meat racks, and truck stops, now home to a medley of expensive clothing stores, art galleries, and restaurants. Lotus, which is where my week had gone wrong, was there, too, but my Mr. Perl drove past it and down under the ancient ruins of the West Side Highway. He squeezed his expensive ride between two long trucks and headed to a red door guarded by two beefy bouncers, neither of whom wore "D" security buttons.

I double-parked near the corner and went over strategy. I didn't know the place. The security didn't belong to D. I was good looking, which always helped. If it was a gay place I was sure they'd let me in. So there was a fifty-fifty chance I'd just walk in.

The odds turned against me when I saw a motley crew of folks in latex, heavy pale makeup, and lots of studded gear jump out of cabs and go inside. My butter-soft leather, charcoal slacks, and turtleneck would not be the height of fashion at this joint. I sat there about twenty minutes. I called D on his cell and got voice mail.

I was thinking about what I'd say at the door when a limo pulled up and out popped Ivy Greenwich, Bee Cole, two lovely black ladies, and a damn near albino rock-star-looking dude. I loved the fact that Ivy and Bee never ever slept. I left the car by the curb, walked quickly over to the doormen, and told them I was there to meet Ivy. Five dollars and a stamp on the knuckles later, I was inside a club where the decor was crimson, candles, and the all-male waitstaff wore studs around their necks.

A stage show was underway. A man and a woman were both tied to life-size wheels. The man was upside down. The woman was sideways. A short, hooded man applied wax, clamps, and the occasional caress to their stretched-out bodies. Trance music rumbled ominously in the background. There were various cameras onstage aimed at various body parts. I assumed there was some kind of live Webcast underway. Some people crowded the stage, but most were chitchatting and drinking. Been there, done that, I guess.

I was wandering the large space in search of familiar faces when someone grabbed my ass. Bee Cole smiled and then kissed me, slipping a tongue between my surprised lips. "My, Night, you are too full of surprises. Are you meeting a client?"

"I was driving by, saw you and Ivy enter, decided to drop by."

"You were just driving by Satan's Dungeon?" she

laughed. "Right, Night. But you are always doing the unexpected."

She took my hand and led me through to another, smaller room where two monitors displayed the onstage action to those seated in reserved booths. In the center of one of them sat Ivy's party, looking droopy-eyed but game. Clearly this posse was out for a night of heavy club crawling, and their journey was likely just half over.

Ivy greeted me like royalty, introduced me to the rock star—some English bloke whose name I didn't catch—and the nubile Nubians. He squeezed me between himself and a fine sista named Flippina.

"Now that I know you didn't kill that woman, your future is made," he announced casually.

"Well, the police have cleared me. I'm free, Ivy."

"That's wonderful. Loved you in Bee's new video and it's just the beginning. Tomorrow you come to my office and sign management papers. With the story you have to tell, the heat over that remix you sang on, and your looks, they'll be printing twenties with your picture on them."

This was all great, of course. But my joy was muted. Ivy could see that. Instead of talking of my search for Mr.

Perl, I switched the topic to Beth Ann. "How's working with her been, Ivy?"

"She's a willful lady," he answered. "Very determined. She's like a damn pit bull when she gets her teeth into something. All she's got to do to help me is to live better. Lots of models eat bad, do drugs, and get caught up in crazy relationships. That's the nature of the beast. I just need minimum clarity. That's all."

"What kind of crazy relationships?"

"Hey, man, you're the one doing her, not me. Besides, I don't spill my clients' business, as you'll see, but just ask around about Beth Ann. It makes interesting listening."

I really wanted to pry but I knew it was uncool, and in fact, as her reputed new lover, not knowing made me look goofy. I was contemplating being honest with Ivy when the "master" who'd been "torturing" the couple onstage headed our way. He was still in full leather-and-chain regalia sans one important item—his mask. It was that same short, stocky, demanding man I knew as Nate Perl. Ivy was about to introduce us when my Mr. Perl recognized me and turned tail.

I must have leaped or crawled over the table, because the next thing I knew I was pushing against the latex and leather of the customers in pursuit of the man who'd ruined my week and almost my life. He was heading toward the stage when I grabbed him from behind. He fell forward onto the lip of the stage. I jumped on his back and punched the back of his head, which probably hurt my knuckles more than his cranium. I put a few more punches on his dome before the bouncers grabbed me.

"He's a murderer!" I shouted as they pulled me off him. The Satan's Dungeon crowd seemed to think this was all part of the gig, but Bee, bless her heart, heard me. As my Mr. Perl tried to climb onstage Bee grabbed one of the onstage chains and whipped it around, smashing the metal into his cheek and sending him sprawling onto the floor. Bee kicked him in the nuts for good measure, then put her brown-leather-booted foot on his neck and shouted, "I know somebody in this motherfucker's got to have some handcuffs!" The Satan's Dungeon crowd applauded appreciatively.

"We Suspect All Kinds of Things"

"We suspect all kinds of things at any given moment, gentlemen," Detective Williams said suavely. "At no point in an investigation are we obligated to share our theories with a suspect or ex-suspect, even one with impeccable references."

I was back in the precinct interview room. Same chairs. Same lighting. Same insufferable dick. Today he was rocking a brown suit, a white shirt, and an impeccable beige tie. The setting was the same as before but the context was so damn different. On this Friday afternoon, I sat with an attorney, Stephen Barnes, Esquire (paid for by Ivy Greenwich), and D. I was no longer the prey. It was Detective Tyrone "Fly Ty" Williams who was on the defensive.

Barnes pressed on. "You could have shown my client a photo of the real Mr. Perl when you had him in custody. That would have saved everyone involved, including you, a lot of trouble."

The detective shrugged. "At the time your client visited

228

with us, we had no reason to believe that there was a man masquerading as Perl. When we canvassed the building, we had no idea that Mrs. Perl was having an affair with her neighbor, Don Mason, a man who we knew to be head of a large insurance company. No one in Mason's daylight world knew he was a part-time sadist.

"The trick is that though they were neighbors, they actually met in an S&M chat room. They'd probably never have started their relationship otherwise. It's also how they found Missy DeMann and Mr. Night's employer. We honestly didn't know who the second Mr. Perl was. Missy DeMann had the same story as Night. Until last night she still thought he was Mr. Perl—at least that's what she says. We can't prove otherwise. The truth is that their affair, and Mr. Perl's employment of Missy DeMann, Mr. Night, and Mr. Enrique Robles, would have continued on if Mrs. Perl hadn't pressed Mason to get a divorce, as she was planning to do. After all their down-low planning, they just fell victim to an old-fash-ioned crime of passion."

When Detective Williams had finished his diatribe, Barnes pressed him some more: "Are you gonna thank my client for being a more diligent detective than you?

My client did the legwork and solved your case, if you hadn't noticed?"

Fly Ty didn't like this way of thinking one bit. "I hardly think a lucky guess is detective work, Esquire. Between fingerprints and DNA and interviewing, we would have found Mr. Mason. And that evidence will be what ultimately convicts Mr. Mason. There's no question about that." He paused, glowered at me a moment, and added, "Still, I appreciate Mr. Night's help, and so does the City of New York. Now, gentlemen, is this grand inquisition over? I have active cases to go work."

This was the moment for a snappy retort. Some nasty yet cool one-liner to put Fly Ty in his place. Yet I had nothing. Guess I wasn't action hero material. All I really wanted to do was get out of that station and get my record deal.

We all stood up. Barnes, D, and I were heading for the door when the detective coughed theatrically and we all turned around.

"Mr. Night, you should tell your Nigerian friend that I've passed his name along to the INS. I thought they might be interested in his many U.S. businesses."

"Fuck the INS," I muttered. "Besides, the man's a citizen."

"What did you say?" the detective demanded.

"You heard me."

D stepped between us. "Let it go, Fly Ty. You got the collar. You get the glory. You're gonna still need my friend to testify. Don't forget that."

Ignoring D's presence, the detective leaned over toward me. "I'll remember you, Mr. Night with an N," he said hoarsely. "Stay out of trouble. Believe me, you don't wanna ever see me again." I stared at this man old enough to be my father and tried to look as hard as I could. Still, D pulled me out of the room with the greatest of ease. He was right. I didn't wanna see him again.

Dreams Do Come True

Dreams do come true. It was Friday afternoon. Gray rain clouds crowded out the sky, and the air outside Ivy Greenwich's office windows was heavy. Ivy himself looked a little weathered. That morning's events at Satan's Dungeon had taken their toll on him. Who knew he'd been managing the phony Mr. Perl?

"We had Mason slated to do a *Real Sex* segment—real-estate mogul by day, sadomasochistic star by night. I'm telling you, the whole thing had exciting multimedia possibilities."

I couldn't really comment on that, so from across his desk I offered, "I guess you'll just have to be satisfied managing me."

He nodded and then signed the last of the papers. He passed them over to me and I signed them as well. Ivy announced that we had a meeting with Power and Walter Gibbs on Monday but added, "We're also gonna meet with Sony, Arista, and Def Jam. We both love the Powerful team, but you're a free agent, Night. You don't work for anyone right now, not even your previous employer. You heard me?"

"Absolutely," I said. "I've been trying to quit that job since I got it. I have some money saved up."

"Please, Night." Ivy reached into his dark mahogany desk and pulled out an envelope. "This should hold you until we make a deal. If you need a ride I can arrange that, too." The check was for $50,000. Not a bad start on my new life.

"This," I said fondling the check, "is of course recoupable?"

"When you get your advance from a label, we take ours off the top and fifteen percent after that."

I smiled and thought to myself, *Hello, my new pimp.* As Ivy talked about the kind of record deal we wanted, my eyes wandered around his office. There were photos of him with Sam Cooke and Teddy Pendergrass. Shots of Ivy in thirty-plus years of fly gear from sharkskin suits to one-piece jumpers to Adidas to the Hugo Boss number he was now rocking. Amid all of the style changes, Ivy had maintained that distinctive, once curly brown, now low and gray Jewish Afro. There was a message in all these images. Styles change, but who you are, the essential you, must remain the same.

"How are you planning to celebrate?" he asked as we headed toward the door.

"I have something to do around nine. After that I'm not sure."

"Join me at Indochine. I'm having dinner with a new signee, a singer-songwriter named Jon Christian, who will be Michael Bolton for post–Backstreet Boys female fans."

I nodded, said, "Maybe," and hoped he wouldn't one day be describing me as "Luther Vandross for post-Usher sistas."

Out in the lobby I got the men's room key from a secretary. It was located out in the hall by the elevators. I went in and relieved myself, enjoying the pee of a contented man. As I was washing my hands I heard the happy flutter of women laughing. I cracked the door open and saw Beth Ann and two other beauties walking toward Ivy's office.

They looked like three long, graceful swans with their svelte torsos balanced on thin, shapely legs. All three wore tinted shades, short jackets (either leather or denim), and either pointy-toed boots or sandals. These women looked like a breed apart, a trio of sisters born of different mothers. If I hadn't come to know Beth Ann, my ass would have been out of that restroom and after her. But I knew her too well. The thrill wasn't completely gone, not yet, but it was mad muted.

I closed the restroom door and looked in the mirror. No matter how far I went in the world, I'd always be that little boy that people thought too dark. I could fight that feeling. I could curse it. I could even sing about it. But that prejudice would always haunt me. Once I'd thought hanging around a woman as fine as Beth Ann or signing with a manager with the power of Ivy Greenwich would unlock that chain. I knew better now. I was still as handcuffed by my childhood as ever.

I went back into the hall and slipped the men's room key under Ivy's front door. I could hear Beth Ann and company inside. I moved over to the elevator and pushed the down button.

I Used to Love It

I used to love it in Raffaella's West Side apartment. It was the place of my apprenticeship, where I'd been molded from a dark piece of coal into a shining black diamond. I looked around the room and told her, "You need to update this place, Rafi."

She nodded agreeably. "I am in the process of redoing everything, Night. Just like you."

"So you're through with the escort business?"

"Eventually, yes." She poured me some jasmine tea. "But unlike you, I do not have a record deal awaiting me. I'll have to make a transition, Night. Before I change my business I have to change my life."

"Which means?"

"I'm going to adopt a child," she said. She paused a bit, as if afraid to speak, and finally added, "I want a boy. A little black boy."

"Okay," I said and tried not to spill my tea. About twenty different thoughts ran through my brain, but all I said was, "That's a pretty radical lifestyle switch, Raf-faella."

"I know, Night, I know." It seemed like she wanted my approval or support, and I wasn't sure I should give it. "But like you, I need new priorities. I know I have to change what's important to me. That night at the vocal teacher's house gave a focus to something I've been feeling for a while. That Ted is such a nice man."

"I think he's gay," I said casually.

But all I did was piss her off. "That doesn't change the fact that he's a nice man, Night," she asserted. "He's got a wife and a lovely child. He's nicer than you, I can tell you that. You're straight and you don't have what he has. So who's the better man?"

"Okay. Okay. I hear you. That was mean and proba-bly not even true."

"Anyway, Ted's place made me see what is missing from my life. I've helped all you street guys and what do I get?"

"Money."

"But that's not satisfaction. Raising a little boy would be challenging but in a really good way. There are so many black boys without homes and mothers, because of drugs. It would be fantastic, Night. Polly is going to help me."

"My client Polly?"

"Our client Polly is on the board of a Catholic child welfare agency. She thinks she can cut through a lot of paperwork for me."

"I hate to be negative," I said, being negative, "but female pimps are not often viewed as ideal adoptive parents."

"Polly believes in me, so I will go forward," Raffaella said decisively. Changing tone, she told me, "She wants you to call her. She says you can still go to museums with her—she doesn't care what anyone says—but she's not paying anymore."

That made me feel good and I told Raffaella I'd call.

"So," she said, "is this it, Night? I won't see you any-more?"

"How could the godfather to your child be a stranger, Raffaella?"

She hugged me and laid her head on my shoulder and teared up. "That would be so sweet," she said, wet eyed. "Maybe I should get married, too, and make a whole family."

This made me nervous, so I joked, "To who? Enrique?"

She sat up with a flushed face and said excitedly, "You think so, too!"

I grabbed her arms and slowed her down. "No, I do not, Raffaella. Listen: one thing at a time, okay? You can't change your life in one day, you know?"

"Okay," she said, "but remember that yourself."

I agreed to do that, gave her a kiss on both cheeks, and headed out the door.

Was Not a Very Good Restaurant

Chinese Empire on Seventh Avenue off Fifty-fifth Street was not a very good restaurant. It served hard brown rice, sugar-heavy sauces, and its drinks were either too weak or too strong. There was nothing to recommend this spot except that it was close to tourist hotels and Adebonojo liked it.

I'd often tried to explain to my African friend that Chinese Empire was a culinary disaster area in a town filled with great Asian cuisine. But my favorite Nigerian was stubborn. Usually I would have put my foot down and made him dine at one of the scores of better Chinese spots in the Apple, but there was no need to beef today. The man had done enough already.

"Why don't you share the shrimp dumplings with me, Night?" he asked politely. "I know you must be hungry."

I declined and took another sip of ginger ale. In the chair next to me was a blue plastic Gap bag filled with twenties and fifties. There was $175,000 inside. He hadn't quite made what he'd predicted, but this was still a nice chunk of money, considering how shaky the economy was.

"The immigration people stopped by the shop," he said, and my heart sank. "Don't worry, Night. All my people have green cards or visas, and I do nothing illegal out of the shop. Most of my activities are as all-American as Bill Gates. All their interest means is that I will not be engaging in any transactions like this in the near future. I'd hate to try to rebuild my business in Lagos."

His friendship with me had put him in danger. I had to protect him as best I could, though I wasn't sure how. As usual, I was relieved when a grim D entered Chinese Empire and took off a beige trench that was damp from the drizzle outside. D sat down, and Adebonojo placed the Gap bag in D's lap.

"Are you hungry?" Adebonojo inquired.

"No, thanks," he said. "An empty stomach makes a mind sharp."

"Indeed," Adebonojo said. "Like Marley said, 'An hungry man is an angry man.' Well, it looks like it's time for me to go. I have watches to sell. Good luck with your transaction. I'm sure I'll be hearing from you." He left a twenty on the table and sauntered out the door. D asked about the INS and I told him what I knew. D shook his head.

"That's fucked," he said. "But I believe I can fix that."

In D's Range Rover, two of his best men, Clarence from Zofia's and Jeff Fuchs from Lotus, sat in the back as we snaked down to Murray Hill. The usually elegant Clarence was dressed like an off-duty transit authority worker, while Fuchs, a wigga from way back, was in Phat Farm right down to his socks. D ran down the particulars to all of us as I smiled and silently prayed.

We cut across Park Avenue in the high Thirties and pulled up in front of a doorman building. I'd phoned Beth Ann on the way, but she still wasn't downstairs. I stood by the front door and waited nervously. The drizzle had ended but the sky was hooded and low, like there was a gray ceiling on the city. I felt troubled and unbalanced. I stood up straight, set my feet firmly underneath me, and swore I wouldn't tip over.

Beth Ann's head was covered in a blue bandanna but otherwise she looked much as she had in the hallway that afternoon. Different clothes, yes, but with that same casual chic. She congratulated me on my deal with Ivy and gave me a deep hug and a moist kiss on the lips. Surprisingly cheerful (maybe it was E?), she told me,

"This is gonna be a great night," and chuckled at her own pun.

Her mood altered when I put her in the passenger seat and she stared at the driver. "Why are you here?"

"The same reason as always," D replied. "To help out a friend." I got in the back and the Range Rover pulled off. Beth Ann turned an angry red face toward me.

"Where's Adebonojo? Shouldn't he be here?"

"We didn't think it was necessary, Beth Ann. They don't know him and they don't need to." I handed her the Gap bag and told her how much was in it.

"We were talking about more than that, Night. Couldn't he get more? If Maura and I had had time I'm sure we could have."

"But," I said, "you didn't. He did what he could. Plus, he took his cut. He doesn't run a charity."

She slumped down in her seat. "It's all gonna go wrong," she mumbled.

"Not," D interjected, "if you've told D the truth and we're properly prepared."

"D," she said, "there's no conspiracy. You can relax your paranoid mind. I just thought introducing them to Adebonojo would show them I couldn't have done it on my own."

"Why did they snatch Maura and not you?" he
asked. "Holding you would have generated a lot more
cash from friends and family."

Beth Ann rolled her eyes at D and let out a bitter
sound that was something between a laugh and a curse.
"They are just like you and everybody else, D. All you
men want the beautiful girl to do for you. All your fucking egos are so small, you need me to make you feel
big. It's such a joke."

D didn't reply. He just wheeled the Range Rover down
Fifth and then made a left on Sixteenth Street. We parked in
a garage and walked toward Union Square. It was seven
o'clock and the sky dark blue, yet despite the earlier drizzle
the park was full of life. People on dates. College kids hanging out. A few skaters on the steps.

The benches in Union Square are long and winding
with round metal bars that separate sections from one
another. D and Beth Ann sat on a bench. I sat on a
metal bar to their right. Clarence lay on the bench to our
left, sprawled out like a bum. Jeff stood further away
near the children's sandbox. D and Beth Ann made
quite a provocative sight—a barrel-chested, bald
brother in an expensive, authoritarian trench coat; a
woman who made fashion editors genuflect; and a wrin-

kled Gap bag squeezed between them. They whispered
to each other—intimate, passionate words I couldn't
make out.

Maura had looked better. Same clothes as five days
before. Hair stringy. No makeup. Unhappy face. The
Israelis were dressed casually so as not to stand out.
Still, there was the empty hardness of death about them.
I'd barely been able to subdue a middle-aged sadist.
What good would I be here if things got ugly? I glanced
at D. He smiled like he knew something.

The short, unpleasant guy led the way with Maura
squeezed between the two gents who'd attempted to
rearrange my pretty face. As they approached, D
tapped the bench and Clarence got up and walked
away (but not far). This made the Israelis very nervous. I
saw them searching all around for suspicious folk. The
guy who'd coldcocked me made eye contact and, without a smirk, rubbed the top of his head. Maura and the
short Israeli guy sat down, and Beth Ann passed the bag
to him. He glanced inside.

"Is that all?" he asked evenly.

"I'm just a girl," Beth Ann said with catwalk attitude.
"Next time, sell your own drugs."

"Who are you?" he said to D.

"I'm her boyfriend," he said and then took her hand. "I also don't like ignorant men manipulating women into doing their dirty work. It's very ungentlemanly. You won't do this again."

The Israeli laughed. "And what would stop me?" he sneered. As they spoke, my two-way buzzed. I shouldn't have taken my eyes off what was transpiring, but I did. The message, in a word, was horrific. It was the worst news of a very bad week. I stood up with a start and all eyes turned my way. I was figuring out the fastest way to Bellevue when a skateboard kid, a woman pushing a stroller, two sets of lovers, and a homeless man all pulled out guns and NYPD badges, rolled up on the Israelis and surrounded Maura, Beth Ann, and D. The Israelis offered no resistance and were quickly cuffed. Beth Ann and Maura embraced. D guided them both away and just like that the little drama was over, like some silly trick of the light.

A scruffy skateboarder/cop had me by the arm when Detective Tyrone Williams walked over. "Let this young man go," he ordered.

"Thank you, sir," I said gratefully.

"And thank you, Night," he said respectfully, "for being a material witness to an arrest of a major ring of Ecstasy dealers. In exchange for your testimony I will help all the recently-minted Americans we know. You understand me?"

"Yes, sir," I said. "Can I go now? I have a family medical emergency." I showed him my two-way message, yet he seemed reluctant.

"It's all right, Ty." D walked up smoking a cigar. He held one up to the detective. "This guy's gonna be a big singer. Bigger than Michael Jackson, R. Kelly, Marvin Gaye, all of them. Believe me. So he'll be happy to give his statement and get on with his career."

"Is this a Cuban?" the detective asked.

D replied, "I have friends in import-export," and handed over the cigar. I saw Beth Ann brushing tears from Maura's face. She felt me looking and turned my way. She blew me a kiss, like I was the camera at a photo shoot. I hated myself for smiling but I did. I'd see Beth Ann again—at Zofia's, at Lotus, at one of the places where vampires gather to seduce willing virgins and sharpen their fangs. I knew she'd be in a back room somewhere, safe behind a door as D stood silently on guard.

I turned from this scene and ran east toward Bellevue. My week wasn't over. There was one more crisis ahead, and I didn't know who would solve it. There was no D or Fly Ty where I was headed.

My Father Sat

My father sat with a *New York Times* in the plastic
chair next to him and my sister's Motorola two-way in
his hands. "This is something else," he told me a couple
of times that night as he read news headlines and sports
scores and played video games on my sister's machine,
as he tried furiously to ignore his daughter's latest medical drama. I didn't have a distraction. I was present and
in the moment. The most intense five days of my life
were ending in pain. My sister was sick again and I was
flashing back, way back.

My mother died at night. She'd been having blood pressure problems since she was
sixteen. Too much pork. Too much stress
between her job, raising Nikki and me, and my
father's endless desire to march, march,
march. Actually, it probably had nothing to
do with Daddy, but I blamed him because he
wasn't there. He was already a mailman yet on
this evening he was out at some meeting, some
last gasp of SOUL. He was trying to breathe

life into a body that had already died, while
we watched her agonize over giving Pepe
Sanchez a B or a C+. I was advocating she
give Pepe a break, and she was gonna let me
read his paper again.

Dr. Morrison was a real comfort. Sensitive and caring, she sat real close to me and my father, explaining what we didn't understand (which was all if it, since only God could truly answer our questions). Ivy paged me three times about dining at Indochine but I didn't have the will to either explain or lie. Though he sat next to me, my father hit me with a message from Nikki's two-way to mine: I LOVE YOU, SON.

My mother fell to her left as she tried
to stand up. Her body took a long slow journey toward the floor. I wish I could have
caught her. I wish I could have moved with a
quickness to grab the body that birthed me.
Instead I cried like the child I was. Nikki
ran in and joined me in tears. Our mother
didn't hear us. She had a stroke in front of
me and died on our living-room rug.

Pops didn't come home until after midnight. He found us all there on the floor.
Nikki and I sat on either side of Ma's body.
He blamed me for not calling an ambulance. I
blamed him for not being where he should have

been. Poor Nikki just got sick. Our family
died along with Ma that night. We didn't pull
together—we fell apart.

Late that night in the Bellevue corridor I thought about
D and Beth Ann and Raffaella and my money lust and
the joyless sex and hoped ('cause who knew what I'd
really do?) that I could turn it all into something good.
Whatever happened next, to my sister, my father, or me,
I knew that I would be different. Not stronger physically.
Not a better singer. Maybe, maybe a better person. I
was being realistic. It was just a chance. It was a small
commitment, but you could build on small things. I'd
hated the way I looked and I'd turned my darkness into
a virtue, so I knew I could change. I could have faith. I
told my father that. He stared at me. He started to type
on Nikki's two-way. I waited for his message. Nothing
came through. I looked over at him and he hugged me,
and I buried my face in his dry gray hair and dreamed
of being a better man.